D0012556

Bárbara Jacobs

THE DEAD LEAVES

translated by David Unger

CURBSTONE PRESS

FIRST EDITION, 1993
Copyright © 1993 by Bárbara Jacobs
English translation © 1993 by David Unger
ALL RIGHTS RESERVED

Cover design by Les Kanturek
Printed in the U.S. by BookCrafters

Curbstone Press is a 501(c)(3) nonprofit literary arts
organization whose operations are supported in part by
private donations and by grants from the ADCO
Foundation, the J. Walton Bissell Foundation, the
Connecticut Commission on the Arts, the Lila Wallace-
Reader's Digest Literary Publishers Marketing
Development Program administered by the Council of
Literary Magazines and Presses, the Andrew W. Mellon
Foundation, the National Endowment for the Arts, and the
Plumsock Fund.

Library of Congress Cataloging-in-Publication Data

Jacobs, Bárbara, 1947-
   [Hojas muertas. English]
   The dead leaves : a novel / by Bárbara Jacobs. — 1st ed.
     p. cm.
   ISBN 1-880684-08-X : $10.95
     1. Title.
PQ7298.2.A33H613   1993
863—dc20   93-7827

distributed in the U.S. by   published by
INBOOK   CURBSTONE PRESS
Box 120261   321 Jackson Street
East Haven, CT 06512   Willimantic, CT 06226

The Dead Leaves

1

Edgar Allen Poe, the Cadillac, and Our House

This is the story of papá, the papá of us all.

Papá's brother's name was Gustav with no "e" after the "v" and he was older than papá. When we were kids, Uncle Gustav was living in Saginaw, Michigan, with an older woman who drank a lot and had a daughter with two kids who had long and sort of straight sandy hair. Uncle Gustav's house was very modern and had lots of things made of wood and smelled like a typical modern American home full of electrical gadgets we didn't know the use of but which worked marvelously. Uncle Gustav worked for a company that made car windshields, but it was his company; it was called Visors Incorporated and was at 2200 Waterfall Street in Saginaw. Uncle Gustav drove a late model Lincoln Continental, usually burgundy-red, with black seats and buttons for lowering windows and raising the front seat or bringing it forward. In front of the garage, he'd press a little button hidden on the dash of the Lincoln and the door would roll up till it was flat against the garage ceiling. Uncle Gustav fell off a horse when he was a kid and that's why he limped a little and didn't hear too well and one of his eyes was sort of half-shut; when he laughed, his lips kind of twisted up to one side. When he was young he began to study medicine, but he gave it up. Around that time he had a girlfriend he was going to marry and who was younger than he and pretty and normal and from the

9

old country, so we were told; the whole family really liked her but nobody knows why he switched to that other one, Mildred, who was fat and didn't always comb her hair. Uncle Gustav never brought Mildred to see Mama Salima, who was his mother — and also father's and Aunt Marie Louise's mother — and our dear old grandma from the States. Another thing that everyone found wrong with Mildred almost at first sight was that she was a Protestant and not even the practicing kind as she never went to any church and never talked to any minister who might've advised her on her drinking problem or how to fix her hair or lose a few pounds. But Mildred's daughter loved Uncle Gustav as if he were her own father, which he wasn't, and everyone said Yes and she'll end up inheriting it all and everyone would get upset, but Uncle Gustav was great to us and we were very fond of him; he gave us radios and pens and anything we wanted, all we had to do was ask. One day he gave us an axe, and he showed us a black and yellow snake in the garden; it made all of the girls among us afraid and made all of the boys among us feel their oats because Uncle Gustav told them to chop off its head. But they didn't because the snake slipped in between the hedges, and while we chased it down, Uncle Gustav followed, filming it and us in color with a movie camera that was the newest model.

Marie Louise was father's and Uncle Gustav's older sister. We called her Aunt Lou-ma. Aunt Lou-ma had lots of thick, black curly hair she let ride down below her shoulders and which actually glowed. By then she had been married four times and was always getting left widowed. Her previous husband sang in church choirs and was even shorter than she and younger and everyone said he wouldn't die and that Aunt Marie Louise wouldn't be widowed again because he was young and strong and had a deep voice, but he died too and Aunt Lou-ma was again a widow, and her children didn't know what music would be sung at the next wedding because at the third he had begged the choir to sing "The Third Man." By her first husband she had had three children who were our first cousins from the States. But we hardly ever saw Aunt Lou-ma's oldest daughter. We heard she had lots of problems because her husband was a heavy drinker. They had about five kids and lived almost hand-to-mouth and our cousin had to struggle, so we heard, to keep the family going. Aunt Lou-ma's first husband had been the son of a Lebanese who'd emigrated like papá and his brother and sisters, and so he was one of us. But Mildred, Gustav's wife, wasn't from the old country, and Mama Salima didn't like that at all.

This oldest cousin's name was Susan. She had so much trouble with her husband that one of her daughters who was about our age or even a bit younger started growing bald. Everybody said that when her parents stopped having problems hair would really start growing on her head again because she'd stop being so nervous.

Bob, our cousin Robert or Bobbie, was next in line after Susan. He was very handsome but very serious and had a nasty temper. Mamá says that he was like papá as a young man, but only in looks. He worked in a general store and used to tell the older boys among us that when they were a bit bigger he would invite them to work for him in the store one summer, then another, and if they caught on they could stay there in Saginaw working with him. We used to give our cousin Bobbie a hard time, just to get his goat. We'd pinch and shove him and eat his share of dessert. And so as not to end up hitting us or losing his temper, he'd pretend he found the whole thing amusing and that his first cousins from Mexico, which is where we were living, were sweet and lots of fun.

But the person we got along with best was Cousin Lisa, the youngest of Aunt Lou-ma's three children. Lisa, short for Elizabeth, but Liza or Liz was also okay. If you considered mamá's brothers' kids as papá's true nieces and nephews — they, like our cousins from the States, were our first cousins — then Lisa wasn't really papá's youngest niece, but he was very fond of her.

Aunt Lou-ma, Susan and Lisa lived in Flint, near Saginaw, and when we went up to visit, they'd either come to see us in Saginaw or sometimes we'd go see them. Aunt Lou-ma and Lisa would come alone because Susan hardly ever left her family behind on account of all the problems. And they'd come to visit Bob, Mama Salima or Uncle Gustav and us — their Mexican family — as well. When Lisa learned to drive, she'd often go to Saginaw by herself to visit Mama Salima and Bob would also often go to Flint to visit his mother and sisters but mamá wouldn't let us go alone with him by car to Flint; that's why we sometimes went by Cadillac from Saginaw to Flint. Flint and Saginaw are both in Michigan, The Lake State, but lakes up there are big as oceans.

Lisa'd tell us some stories about the family. She didn't like blacks because something had happened in the family with a black man and she knew what she was talking about and that things hadn't ended just there. Neither papá nor mamá ever confirmed the story among other reasons because they didn't know we knew about it; we kept kind of secretly waiting for them to tell it to us on their own but they never did. According to Lisa, the daughter of one of Mama Salima's sisters had run off with a black man and had had his child, but he abandoned her and the child, ending up in jail for this or for something else, Lisa wasn't really sure, and this is why Mama Salima never saw her sister ever again, the one who had emigrated to America with her but had gone off to live in some other city in another state of the United States. Lisa used to tell us You don't know what blacks are like because you don't have any in Mexico. We really didn't know if there were or weren't blacks in Mexico, but deep down we had the feeling that if there were, we'd either like them, or not, the way we liked all the people around us not because of their skin color, but for what they were, either mean or nice or whatever.

We all thought that papá felt the same way we did and that he liked blacks if they were nice, and whenever he was with his family in the States all he did was listen because his ideas were already very different from theirs, so he preferred just to listen and lower his head and hardly ever open his mouth.

He'd even do this in Mexico, just drop his head and listen when others talked, even if it weren't about blacks. In Mexico papá also held his tongue but not because of what he heard his own family in the States say.

Uncle Gustav and Aunt Lou-ma liked papá but not all that much. He was always the one visiting them, but they hardly ever visited him in Mexico even though they each wrote I'll do what I can to come down and visit with you this winter. Aunt Lou-ma called papá long-distance each December 20th because she'd remember it was her youngest brother's birthday — papá's birthday. And she'd say sweet things, but when we visited the States we noticed that Aunt Lou-ma and Uncle Gustav seemed to resent papá for abandoning the States and leaving them behind, though he was the one who visited them. That's not the same thing, his big brother and sister seemed to think.

Mama Salima really did like papá and visited him very often in Mexico although mamá would sometimes lose her patience, our house being too small for all of us, but she really loved her mother-in-law, our grandma and the mother of Uncle Gustav, Aunt Lou-ma and papá, and also the great-aunt of papá's second nephew who Mama Salima didn't want to accept because he was half-black.

After all of us had been born, they sent the girls among us to live with mamá's parents in a house that was so big there was even enough room for our sisters to live there. But still, even without the girls in papá and mamá's house there was hardly enough room for the boys, much less for any visitors, though grandma wasn't company but our very dear Mama Salima. What was awful in mamá and papá's house was the men's bathroom which had to be shared with company or family, and just about everybody had to go to the bathroom at the same time; those waiting in the hall for their turn could hear every single sound through the door and, well, that's what it was like.

But Mama Salima's visits to Mexico were a real treat. She'd hole up in the kitchen and make us Middle Eastern pastries stuffed with meat or spinach and no one would see her. She'd fold them differently so you could tell those filled with spinach from those with meat and you'd never get mixed up if there was one kind you didn't like. In Arabic they were called *ftiri* — singular — or *ftaier*, plural.

Mama Salima liked to do three things when she visited her youngest son in Mexico. What she liked most was strolling through the cemetery where she loved the solitude and silence and maybe even imagined the lives of the dead whose tombs she walked between and around; she'd stop at some — not all — to meditate or rest for a while. It was her favorite walk, this wandering alone in the cemetery, and we were told she did the same thing in Saginaw, though she felt something very special in Mexico. She also liked drinking tea in front of the lit fireplace at six in the afternoon, and while she talked in Arabic with my mother's mother, who was Mama Salima's second cousin, she'd smoke and watch the shape of the flames changing as the wood burned. And the third thing she liked to do in Mexico was to sit and read, hour after hour, wherever she happened to be. At times we caught her staring dreamily over her book, probably because whatever she read made her think of something. Papá inherited from her his love of reading.

Mama Salima's favorite book was *Walden* and she lived just like Thoreau since her house was deep in the woods and was the only one for blocks or miles around, just like a ranger's house. Railroad tracks ran down one side of Mama Salima's Saginaw, Michigan house, and when we'd visit her, she'd tell us in the afternoon to go out and wave to the locomotive engineer if we wanted to, and when the train went by and, sure, it would often go by, we'd go out and wave but not stand too close to the tracks. Mama Salima had also read lots of books by Émile Zola, Gustave Flaubert's novels, and many biographies of Napoleon Bonaparte, since she was interested in history and literature, just like papá, but even more interested in the life of Marie Louise, Archduchess of Austria, and Josephine, first a widow, then Empress, and finally scorned and cast aside by the Emperor who divorced her so he could have Marie Louise. Mama Salima read in three languages and spoke them, too, but with different accents, and she wrote in all three languages as well. Mama Salima learned Arabic, then French, and finally English. She learned English in the States when she and her husband moved there at the end of the 19th century and left behind Hasrun, her native city in the Lebanese mountains. But the language she spoke and read most, and she even wrote and published in, was Arabic.

When we appeared on the scene, Mama Salima no longer worked. She had worked a good deal before but now she wrote once in a while for an Arab paper. Before that she had owned a store where she sold Persian rugs, but since she was in the habit of reading behind the counter, she didn't know when customers came into the store or, if she did notice, she'd ignore them because she preferred to go on reading; or else she'd be concentrating so hard she really didn't hear them asking the price of a particular rug or whether the pattern stood for something. She gradually lost customers till in the end it had been best to close the shop so she could read in peace and once in a long while write something for the Arab paper.

We always found Mama Salima in her rocking chair, smoking, with a book in her hands. Her house was piled high with books and newspapers and magazines, but the shelves had mostly books she had taken from Lebanon when she left. Mama Salima had friends who owned farms on the outskirts of Saginaw, and she'd go to them to buy milk and fruits and vegetables and things like that; she loved driving down the highway at low speeds. Her car was an old, light grey Chevrolet, and she'd go plodding down the right lane. She was a Maronite but had learned how to say the rosary in the States and liked it so much that when she visited her friends' farms, the beads would get tangled up in the steering wheel and sometimes Mama Salima would have an accident but never anything serious. Aunt Lou-ma and Uncle Gustav told papá that it was now his turn to tell Mama Salima to stop driving, but papá would answer Let her drive in peace, and never said a word to her about it.

Papá had left the States many years earlier and was quite different from his brother and sister.

In Mexico papá owned the Hotel Poe on Edgar Allan Poe Street, Number eight. He had lots of shelves full of books in his office on the first floor, just like at home.

Whenever he took us to the hotel he'd bring us to a stone fountain that had a giant on top, only lying down. No water came out of the fountain so we could walk all over the giant, who lay face up, without worrying about drowning but only about falling, though it was a short fall and papá was there to pick us up. But he rarely brought us to either the hotel or the fountain. Just once in a while. And the youngest of us, the one with papá's name, never even had a chance to go to either one because papá had grown tired of bringing us or maybe he thought we'd become bored of always going with him to the same two places we liked more than anything else in the world.

The youngest of us missed out on many of the trips we'd take with mamá and papá in his Cadillac. We traveled a lot because both papá and the Cadillac were from the States and had to renew their papers when their permission to stay in Mexico was up, and they'd have to cross the border to fix and renew everything to keep from being hunted down by the local police for being in Mexico illegally.

We had to have some of our meals in restaurants on the highway because mamá would stuff a big old basket with just the first meal which we'd have whenever we felt hungry after leaving the house at kilometer x on the highway north. And depending upon where we were going, we'd have to spend the night in motels, sometimes one night, sometimes four or five nights, depending on the weather or how far we were going or if papá was tired and wanted to rest so we could go on our way the following day without his being too sleepy and running a risk. And sometimes if we went by the house of a friend of papá's, we'd spend the night there. Papá, being in the business, was always given a discount at motels, but he preferred friends because there were so many of us; even if his friends' houses were big, we didn't mind sleeping in sleeping bags on the floor. In those days we weren't scared that someone would stumble over us in the dark and kill us or that the heating system would break down and we'd all die choked by the gas or that someone hadn't put out the fire completely and a spark would somehow fly off and land on a curtain and set it on fire and that then the whole house would go up in flames, including the wooden floor we were sleeping on, and that our sleeping bags filled with feathers would catch fire easily.

When we ate at roadside restaurants or sometimes with papá's friends in their homes, he would put mustard on the hot dogs or ketchup on the hamburgers, and if any of us put ketchup on the hot dogs or mustard on the hamburgers, papá would say we were know-nothings or not connoisseurs like him, but he'd say it without getting mad because he rarely ever did.

Back then papá hardly ever got angry, only when mamá took her sweet time getting out of the house for our long trips, because he really liked to drive the car and he wanted to set off as soon as possible. Very early in the morning he would warm up the engine of the Cadillac and wait behind the steering wheel in the dark to head out, with the suitcases already in the trunk; in the meantime, mamá went on puttering around the kitchen putting together the basket of food or telling the cook and the maid and everyone else in the world what they had to do each day while we were on our trip, things like washing the windows real good or not forgetting to water the garden and all those other things she was constantly reminding them of, only with more insistence when we were about to set off on a trip and, in the end, papá would lose his patience. And if the youngest of us was staying behind with the nursemaid, mamá would take even longer getting out because she kept going back to kiss our youngest brother and all this drove papá berserk and made him honk the horn in the morning darkness and for once papá would blow his top.

But once we were on the road and he'd start smelling the food in the big basket and get hungry, he'd begin to smile and say Yum-yum to make mamá smile too and say It's time to eat and put everyone in a good mood and papá would stop the Cadillac so we could eat at the side of the road. In Arabic this roadside meal was called *zwedi*.

Those were happy times.

Papá had many friends in Mexico but only a few were Mexican; almost all of them were Poles or Italians or from the old country and they'd speak English among themselves, most of the time playing bridge at home or in some club. Once papá told mamá that a Chinese general from Chiang Kai-shek's side had gone to play with them at the club and that he hadn't liked that very much, and we remembered it because it was one of the few times papá explained something when we were still small. When his friends played cards with papá at our home, they'd take off their jackets and smoke. A cigarette or cigar dangled from their lips and the ash would hang in the air till it broke off like a drop of water from a power or a telephone line and fell by its own weight, crumbling on the green felt tablecloth though mamá had placed ashtrays all about. And papá's friends and papá too would keep an eye always half-closed while they played because of the rising smoke or as a kind of ploy or to look more like real gamblers.

All of us girls were in love with some of papá's friends, each with a different man and then we'd switch off so that we could all mentally have a turn with each friend, but none of them even noticed or paid much attention, maybe because they knew we girls were too young and they could get into hot water and lose papá as a friend if something happened, but nothing ever did. Their names were Beco, Ed, Sohn, and so on. They would roll up the sleeves of their shirts, which were almost always striped, and some of them wore suspenders and had a bit of a belly.

With the one papá called The General, but who wasn't Chinese, he'd play chess not bridge, face to face without talking, silently hunched over the playing board on the rectangular wooden dining table to which mamá would sometimes add two end-leaves so that fifteen or more of us could sit around it. The General called us little bastards under his breath but papá or mamá never heard him. He'd call us little bastards because if we were skating or bicycling or playing marbles in the courtyard by the front door when he'd come and ring the buzzer, we wouldn't open the door if we saw through the peephole that it was him. Then the gardener or the driver would have to run to open the door, and when he came in and walked past us he would say Little bastards without even looking at us. The General always asked to borrow books from papá just like Aunt Sara would. And papá would lend them to him because he was a nice guy and expected to have them returned to him and even when they weren't returned he wouldn't get angry because he liked his friends and he'd never get angry, well almost never.

Though the boys among us attended an American school and the girls among us went to a French school where many of the classes were in English anyway, papá insisted we learn his language best of all. He'd make us study it even more in the late afternoon with a teacher named Eugene Fisherman, though when she signed the column she wrote every day for the newspaper *Excelsior* that grandpa subscribed to, she signed it Eugenia Pescador. Papá also lent books to Eugene Fisherman or Eugenia Pescador, and she always returned them but with book covers that papá took off as soon as she left because they made noise when you touched them and would give papá goosebumps like we got whenever Eugene Fisherman's nail or chalk had a way of scratching the board she used to write on to help her when it was time to teach us English.

When papá talked to us he did it in English.

Papá hardly spoke to us, and he'd grow very exasperated with the one of us who talked too much and who as a child was always saying like the rest of us I'm bored, and papá would always say Sshh to him from his armchair without lifting his eyes off the book he was reading since he was always reading. That brother of ours, the one who talked a lot, stuttered when he was bored and one night when we were in a hotel dining room in Oaxaca he stuttered so much that papá first lost his patience, then got angry and said to him Stop eating and talk, and we all started laughing as did those people sitting at the other tables who we didn't even know;

papá grew even angrier and he was ready to stop eating and get up from the table, but he got a hold of himself and little by little he ate everything he was about to leave uneaten or half-eaten on the plate even though he had picked all that he liked best on the menu. Whenever he lost his temper, he'd control it at dinner and leave his plate clean.

Mamá would tell us to do like papá who never left a crumb on his plate. And that papá had learned not to leave anything because he had been to war and knew what it was like to go hungry. We knew almost nothing about any war, and we had never been hungry, but we began to find out more about wars by watching TV than from the schools we went to. Papá bought a set as soon as the first ones went on sale, and as we grew up we started to see war movies where both sides ended up killing one another without even having the time to be hungry. We didn't know which war papá had been in and on whose side, or if he had been a hero, but we thought so even if he never told us. And one day the youngest of us got up enough nerve to ask mamá if papá had won or lost the war in which he had been hungry and mamá had to tell him the truth, I mean part of the truth because first our brother had asked on which side had papá fought and she had answered On the good guys', and then when she had to answer if he had been with the winners or the losers, she had had to say The losers, and our brother asked How was that, if he had fought with the good guys. It was clear that he had gone hungry and from then on he never left a crumb on his plate and instead of eating two of the almond cookies mamá made, he would eat four or five.

23

Papá had been a buck private in the U.S. Army before marrying mamá and then for two or three years afterwards. On one of the trips we took they brought us to visit the camp where papá had been stationed; it was called Tinker Field but we didn't see anything or hear any bugles. It was in Oklahoma City and there we also saw the home where papá and mamá lived as newlyweds but only from the outside. The door was green and we stood gawking at it so long that we saw a hand or the fingers of a dark hand draw open the curtains of a window next to the green door to see who was standing out there watching. We got back into the Cadillac, and papá pressed down on the gas and the green door and Tinker Field stayed behind us forever since we never went back. We stretched our arms and our hands from the back seat where we knelt, and we laid our chins like dogs on the backrest, but we didn't reach a thing and everything slipped away and stayed behind.

One day mamá gave us the khaki-colored scarf from papá's soldier's uniform. And one day she gave us another of papá's scarves from when he had been in the war. This one didn't itch our necks so much when we passed it around to bring us good luck when things were tough like when we had final exams. It was made of silk while the khaki one was of itchy but cuddly wool. The silk one was red with little gold figures and a red and gold fringe; it was quite worn and mamá'd say Soon I'll mend it but she never did. She had no time because she was always baking papá's favorite cookies, and she loved it whenever he was happy and didn't get angry. And also she couldn't mend it because we wouldn't give it back to her. We were afraid she'd keep it and put it away in a drawer she kept under lock and key and where she stored her secrets which all had to do with papá; one of us had discovered it — the one we affectionately called Lo — because as time went by he became more of a locksmith. One day he had unlocked the drawer, and we had seen papá's letters to mamá and hers to him and an album with papá's photos of the war mamá was always talking about.

In those pictures neither papá nor any of his buddies wore any army's uniform though they all wore espadrilles even when it was winter and there was snow. In one shot papá's buddies are leaning against a tank with rifles on their shoulders while papá seems to be sitting with a newspaper spread across his lap as if he'd like to read it in peace once they're done taking the war photo.

When papá got real angry he'd go to his room and lock the door.

Papá slept naked, and we'd see the soft down under his armpits because before dozing off he'd read for a long time and curl one arm, laying it on the pillow under his neck. He had a silk robe he'd put on for breakfast, and he'd never close it well and mamá was always telling him with a little cough Cover yourself up, in a whisper so we wouldn't hear, but it was so the females among us or the nanny or the cook wouldn't look, if they happened to come into the dining room and see him.

Papá would light a fire in winter and he'd sit in front or on the side of the fireplace to read his books, his magazines or his bridge manuals, and if one of us left the door open papá would get angry because the heat would escape. Damn! he'd shout, because the fireplace was in the foyer and everyone even the dog was always coming in and out; many of us would often forget to close the door and when we'd remember papá had already let out his Damn!

He also got angry and said Damn! when we got a new puppy after the old doggy had died because the puppy wouldn't be able to protect a thing and he'd just go around making pipi all over the house or in our laps and papá would say I don't want that dog in the house after saying his Damn! and then head off to lock himself up in his room. The puppy was a reddish brown little fluff ball nice and warm and sweet and when he was brought to us on November 20th, practically the day he was born, we named him Maxwell Harrison Finnigan Apricot Pepe Alvarez, but we called him Maco unless we got real angry at him, and then we'd call him by his full name so that he'd tilt his head and straighten his ears out right and look puzzled for a while. At first papá didn't care for Maco but in time he began to like him and would throw him the ball and play with him and would even let Maco go with him into the yard if papá felt like reading outside under an orange tree.

Before Maco we had Terry who was a boxer and before Terry a mutt named Blackie; papá had really liked these two from the start, especially Blackie because he was black and just a mutt. We'd also had a fine pedigreed dog who we named Mister Collins and who'd go along with us without making a fuss or barking when we cried. One day we painted Blackie white with wet lime using a brush that tickled but didn't make him laugh and when papá saw him he got angrier than ever, sort of. This time we were punished, a few of us put in one room and the rest in another, but we still were able to communicate with one another using all kinds of tricks we learned that day and not only never forgot but actually perfected. Soon, almost immediately after that, Blackie died.

The real punishment would've been if they had locked us up in papá's closet; it was quite small and would've been a real jail if mamá had known how to lock it. One of us figured out a way to jam the handle of papá's closet against the handle of their bedroom door and there was no way for the prisoner to get out and escape. That's how we got to know papá's closet from up close and to touch and smell all the things in it. Papá had almost no clothes so it wasn't so hard to know what he kept in the closet because he never hid any secrets under his shirts like mamá did in her drawer, or maybe just an almond cookie which he could secretly devour in the middle of the night, but if whoever of us got locked in there discovered it, he would also secretly eat it before papá got his chance and the lock-up would actually become a feast.

Those were happy times.

The motto of papá's hotel was A Home Away From Home, and when papá wasn't at home he was in the home away from home as if he too were a traveler. He invited a few hotel guests to the house in the beginning but then he stopped. When he invited them again it was for New Year's Eve when papá had lots to drink and lots to say, and he'd begin to stutter he laughed so hard; he and his friends would even break a piñata, which those who were foreigners passing through had never seen, and they'd be in stitches as mamá blindfolded them, and made them dizzier than the champagne, the wine, and the toasts had certainly made them, and she'd hand them a stick and tell them not to peek but to try and swat the piñata; it was always a chicken or a bull or a witch or whatever mamá would find in the market so they'd have fun smashing it and be surprised to have falling on their heads tons of candies or cigarettes or peanuts in their shells or matchbooks from papá's hotel with the motto A Home Away From Home in English.

But one of our uncles wouldn't wait for the piñata. He just stayed long enough to drink glass after glass of champagne with papá, and then he'd leave because he didn't want to ruin his imported English cashmere suits and also because he claimed that papá's friends were Communists just like papá, and he didn't want to hang around with them too long since he wasn't a Communist. Papá would ask him to stay, and that's when our uncle would tease him for not being able to talk Oxford English like he did, and he'd drink another glass of champagne and shake his index finger at him and again call papá a Communist because he had once gone to Cuba for a hotel owner's convention, invited by Fidel Castro, and papá had been charmed by Havana and thought Fidel was a swell guy. All of us had seen him and his men on television come down from the mountains with rosaries around their necks and thick, curly beards, and papá smiled so hard he was almost crying or so it seemed to us watching him.

Still our uncle was awfully fond of papá and papá of him even if he called him a Communist and papá didn't have any suits or an accent from an English university. And on New Year's Eve papá would wait for this uncle to arrive before uncorking the first champagne bottle and he was always the first to come, before it actually turned dark, early in the evening.

Another friend of papá's would mark his arrival by throwing a handful of firecrackers and Roman candles from outside the gate, and later he'd be the first to do cartwheels in the living room after the meal and before and after someone had broken the piñata hanging on a thick cord tied from a terrace beam to a tree in the yard. Usually this friend who did cartwheels rested his head on Aunt Sara's legs because he almost always rolled over toward her, mamá said, because Aunt Sara's knees were smooth and she had given up wearing underwear ever since she had had to put up with the unbearable heat of southern Mexico where she had lived, long before she decided to translate mystery novels on a black typewriter. Still you couldn't see anything.

Aunt Sara got along real well with papá because she was always coming to the house to ask him for help on her translations. When she couldn't figure out some mysterious phrase, she'd ask papá, who loved to tell her what it meant. Sometimes he and mamá would visit Aunt Sara at her place. Her house was very tiny and pretty and full of light and warmth and plants and delicate porcelain knickknacks, some of them from Lebanon, for she was from there too. To get to her house you had to climb a narrow spiral staircase and bear the cold wind gusts because Aunt Sara's apartment was on the top floor of a very tall building. She had her typewriter at the far end of a smallish table also used for eating or for stacking the recently washed, ironed, and impeccably folded bedsheets and pillow cases for the marriage bed where Aunt Sara had slept alone since her divorce.

Sometimes the males among us stared at her knees trying to get a peek at something more, but they never did; Aunt Sara may have been divorced and may have had strange underwear habits, but she was proper and always kept her legs close together under her tight always black skirt. Papá was really quite fond of Aunt Sara and when a few days had gone by without a call or a visit from her, he would say to mamá Call her up and ask her how she is and when she's coming over, and mamá would do it, for she was also quite fond of Aunt Sara and didn't feel that her presence made mamá jealous.

Papá didn't like music, but that didn't keep him from buying a record player. On New Year's Eve, he put on record after record for his friends to shake and dance till the wooden slats under the rug gradually loosened, and from that time on they squeaked even when nobody danced or did cartwheels, but simply walked or stepped on them.

Papá enjoyed listening to both sides of a calypso music record. He liked the way the black men from Nassau sang and pounded on the piano and the drums and he'd always put on that record New Year's Eve even if he never danced to it. Mamá danced, but he would never.

Once mamá told us about the time papá put on his only suit for a special dinner and took her out to dance, but halfway to the dance floor he had stopped and stayed there smiling because he didn't like to dance and he didn't like parties, only his own, the New Year's Eve party in his house with his friends and buddies.

Papá liked black people a lot and that's why we thought he would enjoy meeting his nephew once removed who was half black and roamed God knows where in the world and who most probably was charming and smart even if our cousin Lisa claimed that wasn't possible. If papá had heard her maybe he wouldn't have dropped his head and kept quiet; he'd have told her to shush even if she was his niece and he liked her and was also fond of her not just for being white and family but sweet and smart though full of prejudice.

On the first of January, papá would be quieter than usual and he'd spend most of the day in his room but not under lock and key as if he were angry which he wasn't. Mamá would say that maybe he had a headache or something because her own back was hurting from all the cooking and her legs from all the dancing. And in the morning the house would be full of champagne corks and confetti and popped balloons. The older ones among us pretended to be grownup; they hung out with the adults at the party as if they were also adults and papá would get so confused he'd end up giving them champagne. Well into the night the youngest among us would roll out of bed in pajamas and sneak silently down the hallway and join mamá and papá's dressed up friends without being seen and hide behind a couch where the corks from the champagne bottles always landed; they'd gather these into little heaps and pass the tips of their tongues over them to sneak a taste of the champagne that was always there and which they were now tasting for the first time.

It was like the oil painting of papá which hung over mamá's side of the bed and which she had painted from memory while he was in boot camp and she had lots of free time and was so much in love with him. Papá's painting had always hung there but still we were only now getting to know him a little at a time even if we knew that picture by heart and dreamed about it. Mamá slept with a pillow over her head so the rays of the lamp that papá read by wouldn't bother her, but the first thing she did when she awoke was to throw off the pillow and see papá's portrait, which was always in that place all through our childhood.

One night the one of us who had been awakened by voices and was brave crept up to the living room. He didn't go in but from outside the open door he heard papá and mamá talk and even cry over the things they were discussing. Papá was telling her that he was a bad father since he hadn't had a father and that he didn't know how to be a good one, just how to be the kind he was; then mamá said she was a poor mother because all of us had turned out like him not her and that she also didn't know how to be a good mother because each one of us had been suspended briefly from school and that very day the youngest had been sent home and she thought that it was the last straw; she didn't like the way things and the whole situation were turning out though we felt everything was just fine. We were happy and liked our papá and mamá a whole lot and had never asked ourselves if they were good or bad even if they were different from each other and different from other parents we knew and with whom we, naturally, compared them. Papá and mamá were different, especially papá, but we had never asked ourselves if he was a good or a bad father, and we really liked him a lot, though we didn't know him all that well because he hardly talked to us.

We loved mamá and papá very much, though we didn't know him as well as her because we didn't spend that much time with him, and he never had much to say.

Papá, who didn't like to go to the movies, said that the only film worth seeing was *The Treasure of the Sierra Madre*. When he took us to the movies he stayed in the lobby reading though he had bought a ticket and it was like throwing money away. But once we saw a picture where Bette Davis acted like a little girl who raised the hem of her skirt and with a finger almost in her mouth began to sing a song which went like this I wrote a letter to papá up there and I told him Dear Papá I need you, but when our sisters acted like even younger girls and sang it, they would add Dear Papá I love you and Dear Papá I miss you, and to all of us it seemed that this was a picture that was worth something, though papá hadn't seen it, and so we couldn't know what he'd have thought of it, though from all he read we always thought his opinion would have been the right one.

One day papá brought to the house a chauffeur to drive mamá's car and take us to school and mamá to visit her friends and do her shopping so she wouldn't get so tired out. His name was Adalberto and he was from the north, a Protestant, but papá liked him and often said You should attend the university, Adalberto; well, then Adalberto began taking afternoon classes and he would let us look at some of the illustrations in the books papá bought for him to study. We were horrified to see body parts — Adalberto was studying medicine — and he'd leave the groundkeeper's light on until late at night till he got his degree and went back up north to open his practice after thanking and saying goodbye to papá who told him Write to me, my friend, and you'd better stop by and visit us and not forget us and Adalberto came to our house from up north on New Year's Eve to share a few drinks with papá and to let him know how his life was going.

After Adalberto, came José who later became a traffic cop and when he came back to visit he had a gold ring with a ruby-like stone set in the center. He came with motorcycle boots and badges sewn on his uniform, and, if papá wasn't home, he showed the males among us how to drive, but never on New Year's Eve, because on that day he would act as if he were too important to fool around with kids, even if the kids themselves went around that day acting as if they were grownups too.

Sometimes papá would go by himself on trips to see his family or his friends, but he wasn't afraid to go alone on an airplane because he'd be able to read in peace. Mamá, on the other hand, was very scared of flying but told us that when she felt sure the plane was going to crash — she had seen a tiny wisp of smoke slipping from a crack on one of the wings — all she needed to do was turn and look at papá next to her, and if he were reading that was enough to calm her down. She said that while he was reading, there couldn't be any sort of danger, and then she'd sink back in her seat comfortably for the rest of the flight.

When papá returned from his trips, he'd bring gifts, and once he brought Chinese blouses for the girls and Chinese caps with a red star for the boys, and mamá gave the boys permission to wear the caps, but she wouldn't let the girls wear their blouses for a long time because she said I don't know who helped him choose the right sizes. She was extremely jealous. Papá poked fun at her jealousy and her odd ways, like the night she snatched away the book papá was reading in bed and flung it with all her might, teeth clenched, against the wall so he would stop reading and listen to what she was saying. Papá couldn't stop laughing, and he got up with his closed robe to pick up the book and he found the page where he'd been and went on reading, shaking a bit in laughter as if nothing had happened.

But when mamá went on a trip with grandma, not with papá and not by plane, he took the opportunity to check himself into a hospital and be operated on, we never found out for what, and he stayed there alone and only mentioned it to the oldest male among us should anything happen to him, but all he did was read in peace till the doctor finally said You can go home now, and he came back.

Papá's books had illustrated labels inside the covers with his and mamá's name even if she never read them, but her own books, cookbooks, didn't have a separate label with just her or his name. The illustration was in black and white and had a book open to the middle on a lectern upon a small old wooden table next to a cheerless candelabra with a candle just about to die out.

Mama Salima's books also had labels with her name, but hers were in color and had a boy sitting pensively on the shore looking out at an island with a castle the tips of whose towers merged with the clouds. Mama Salima kept on her night table a book on opera, next to *Walden*, though we never heard music nor saw a record player in her house.

Papá and mamá are second cousins, but they resemble each other only in their eating habits and in some other ways. But in general, they have nothing in common; in fact, they are very different, one from the other, like in religion, which papá doesn't believe in. One time when we were visiting some of his friends in Dallas, Texas, his friend asked one of us at suppertime to say grace, and our brother didn't want to or couldn't; mamá got very angry and felt embarrassed in front of our hosts for how poorly educated we children were, but papá on the contrary wasn't angry because it had seemed altogether natural for our brother to have refused to say grace. In this way, they were different, papá from mamá, and it sometimes forced our souls to be divided into two not very equal halves, but this division was superficial and fleeting, and our souls would come back together in an instant, and not a trace of separation remained, at least, that's how it seemed to us who at that time were, yes, it's true, very happy.

Papá had what's called a steadfast character while mamá not so much. We knew that if he liked, for example, almond cookies, he really liked them, but we didn't know whether mamá would like something she had liked before; this time she might not like it, we were never sure even if we knew her better, a lot better, than papá and that's why we said — but only among ourselves — that her character in contrast was weak or fragile or unstable or volatile — that is, fickle, capricious, changeable, according to most definitions — not that we really cared, but that's the way she was.

And it's not as if she liked to do certain things — maybe she didn't like doing them but did them anyway — well, she seemed to like doing them, but with her you never knew, her character being so volatile, while with papá, though you might not know what he thought, you somehow knew where he stood.

One time a friend of mamá's convinced her to do something that perhaps she didn't want to do, but she went ahead and told us I'll be right back, and she went with her friend and what happened was awful. Mamá had gone off to color her hair and it came out dreadful, and we were so shocked because we remembered what had happened to Blackie — the dog we had painted white and who died almost right away after that — but papá wasn't shocked, and he reacted the same way he had when we had painted Blackie, and he had become angry and shouted Damn! and tightened his lips that way and shouted Damn! and shaken his head this way, and our souls had started dividing into two not so equal halves, and this time we thought they would stay that way, with a rift between the parts, and there was no possible bridge capable of ever joining them, but this wasn't what happened; these were just fears that we ourselves had dreamed up that had a way of taking shape and building up and who knows how it would all turn out.

One never knew. Many things would happen and soon stop happening, but one never knew if soon they'd happen again and papá liked the suspense, just like in the mystery novels he read as a break from reading the historical, literary, and political books he normally read. But we didn't like it; on the contrary, it made us edgy, and in fact one of us had so many nightmares he began sleepwalking. Often he would sit up in his bed with his blue eyes wide open, spread out his arms and say Take care of my children, as if he were papá going away and leaving us to be cared for by someone else. He's asleep mamá would say, begging us not to laugh and not to remind him the following morning of what had happened, but we thought What if it happens again, and we were scared, because really one never knows.

For example: years ago, when we were a lot younger and we all fit into one room piled on top of one another in cradles and beds and cots and even on the floor, papá and mamá would invite friends to spend the night, even if it wouldn't be all that comfortable especially since we had just one bathroom. And then when they sent the girls among us to live with our grandparents, mamá's parents, they still had friends staying over in the house in spite of everything. But one fine day they said Enough is enough, and from then on Mama Salima was our only guest though mamá suffered through it because we lacked space, or perhaps once in a while an old friend of papá's stayed — it had to be a very good friend like Jack. But really it wasn't because we didn't have room for visitors or that papá preferred his friends to stay in his hotel: it all had to do with the last visitor they had and what happened. Her name was Rose and her last name was Dustt, dust but with a double "t," because one wasn't enough.

Rose Dustt was something of a close neighbor of Mama Salima in Saginaw and had a large family, a huge house and a doctor husband who had built his life around his grandfather's one really bad experience. The grandfather of Rose Dustt's doctor husband was also a doctor who had had the bad luck to have someone knock on his door very late one night, and, since he was a doctor and a fellow human being, he opened the door to see who it was and what was going on. He found a wounded man asking for help, and he, the grandfather of Rose Dustt's doctor husband, attended to him like a doctor and a fellow human being only to learn later that the straggler he had let in and helped was none other than the fleeing killer of President Abraham Lincoln, and this, as one would expect, had caused a furor.

That was a pretty good story because, as expected, it was full of suspense like some of the books papá read. We passed the time wondering whether the grandfather of Rose Dustt's doctor husband had done right or wrong or what he might have felt upon learning who it was he had helped, but everything in life has its limit, and each time Rose Dustt came to Mexico she would stay in our house, and after telling mamá and papá the new details that her husband had managed to uncover or figure out about his grandfather, she'd say Let me show you pictures of Mama Salima, and out would come the screen to project her slides. We'd sit on the floor, on the rug that covered the slats of the living room floor, to see the pictures that Rose Dustt had brought from Saginaw for us to enjoy, and then what made mamá and papá say Enough is enough happened, and hardly ever again did they have visitors staying in the house.

What happened was that Rose Dustt showed us 364 slides of her family and finally, at the end, one of Mama Salima sitting alone in the woods on a garden chair, and we didn't feel that this was fair and papá said Damn! after Rose had gone into the guest room to sleep, a room that mamá herself had prepared for the visit, while we all suffered through Rose Dustt's stay in Mexico with twice or three times as many discomforts, especially since we had just one bathroom.

But the door was always open to Jack since he was papá's good friend and if it hadn't been for Rose Dustt, he would've continued putting up his closest friends in the house, no matter what discomforts the lack of space brought.

Every once in a while Jack would visit papá in Mexico. He was an old friend; his last name was Carpenter, and he had a jaw like Popeye's, and he traveled by car with a thermos, a flashlight, binoculars, maps, compasses, tools, and an emergency medical kit, while we traveled only with a thermos. We liked him a lot, a whole lot. Mamá would tell us that Jack was a very old friend, and that he had been the one with whom papá had gone off to war and that's why they had so many things to talk about, and we shouldn't make any noise nor barge in on them or interrupt them because they spent time remembering things from the war where they had almost starved and had worn espadrilles, according to the pictures we had secretly seen in the album mamá kept under lock and key as her very personal treasure.

All this leads up to the time when we each began to grow more and more curious to find out all about that "earlier" life of papá's. We had grown a little tired of imagining what had happened in his life and getting suspended from school every so often, although unfortunately only briefly, for more or less telling the truth of what happened to him. We were very fond of papá, even if he got angry at us and wouldn't talk to us and spent all his time reading or playing bridge with his Italian and Polish friends or chess with that little bastard of a General who with his kind of talk ended up corrupting ours during our childhood.

The moment came when we passionately sought information about papá, and once when papá and mamá said to us We're going, we said fine as long as they wrote to us at least once a week, and mamá said I'll make sure of that, and they went off to Europe.

They visited several countries, many actually, though it isn't important to mention which, only that they didn't go to Spain, because papá had said that it still wasn't the right time to go to Spain. And so it was from Rome that mamá first began to keep her promise of writing to us and that first news did satisfy part of our curiosity and eagerness to learn more about papá.

Mamá mentioned that one day while she and papá were drinking a glass of wine in an open-air café in Rome, she had seen Greta Garbo at the table next to them. When she told him Look it's Greta Garbo, he looked over and had said No, it can't be and the more mamá insisted, the more he doubted, and she had ended up asking other tourists sitting at nearby tables and though they nodded and swore to papá that it was she, he said It can't be, because he had a steadfast character. Mamá wrote to us that he was a skeptic just like Greta Garbo whose only wish was to be left in peace, though in papá's case he wanted to read in peace and recall his earlier life in peace though the earlier part was the war.

All right. So papá wanted to read and that was fine with us, but he also did other things besides play bridge or chess or take care of his guests in the hotel or the home away from home.

Papá also liked to swim, for example, and we enjoyed the way he did it because he'd go swim before the sun came out or had already set so he wouldn't get burned, though when he drove on the highway, he would drive with the window down and his left arm exposed. He was a good swimmer and the females among us were even a bit scared that he would swim too far off with his long, smooth strokes as if he were a professional swimmer, and we said Papá's going to get lost, and from the shore we would stick a finger in our mouths and act like little girls and cry out to him Papá dear, we need you, Papá dear, we love you, Papá dear, we miss you, so that he would come back, and when he did we would give him a towel and he would say Thanks, girls, in English just before going under the overhang of the terraza and starting to read in peace facing the waves and the sea and the sand in which we buried our fear of his getting lost in the water.

Papá was all man, and the girls among us who were half in love with papá's foreign friends said that if among them they could find one man like the one in the oil painting mamá had painted of papá from memory she was so in love with him, they would have fallen in love with that man because they couldn't fall in love with papá, it just couldn't be.

And the girls among us who couldn't be in love with papá because that couldn't be were jealous of one particular friend of papá's. Her name was Barbara and she lived in Manhattan and mamá wasn't jealous of her because she said That's in the past.

Every New Year's Eve almost always the phone would ring about halfway through the evening and almost always it was a long distance call for papá from New York. It was his friend Barbara with the hoarse voice calling and mamá always said Barbara's already "feeling happy" when she answered and passed the phone over to papá. All around him there were balloons and champagne and his friends were talking and dancing and doing somersaults in the living room while he answered the call from his old friend Barbara. We always heard papá tell her more or less the same things and these things had to do with his promise not to forget anything of what had happened before, and he swore he really did remember and would always remember what had gone on before.

Mamá told us that Barbara had been one of papá's old girlfriends when he had lived in Manhattan and had been young and had had many girlfriends and not just one as when she had been his girlfriend. And she told us that Barbara had gone with him into the bookstores and libraries of New York because way back then papá already spent his time reading and had been more interested in that than in having a family which he later wanted when he had met her, mamá, who to him had been someone special.

But one New Year's Eve, Barbara failed to call and even mamá was a bit concerned, and she grew even more concerned and papá did too when Barbara didn't call from Manhattan the following New Year's Eve nor the one after that. And that's why when the phone rang the following New Year's Eve in the middle of the night halfway through the party, mamá ran to answer, and she was happy to hear Barbara's hoarse voice, and she turned sad when she heard her crying and she quickly called papá who was talking even stammering with his friends and drinking champagne with them, and mamá said to him Hurry up Barbara is already "feeling happy" but she sounds bad to me, and papá could do nothing less than to promise Barbara never to forget what had happened and swear he would always remember the past and that's when one of us picked up the extension and heard Barbara say to papá with the hoarse voice mamá said she had because she was already "feeling happy" that she needed him and loved him and missed him, which was the way things were, and that we understood so very well because we too felt exactly the same way.

2

From a Persian Rug to the Other Side of the Border South of the United States of America

"I was going to be the greatest writer! I didn't have a book published yet, but I was going to be a great writer. I wrote about theater. What did I know about theater? Nothing! But I wrote about everything and anything: chess, dancing, music!"

Emile Jacobs

Well, finally the moment arrived for us to start finding out what this earlier life of papá's was all about, when he was a young man before he married mamá and even before he became a buck private in the U.S. Army; we more or less knew about his army life and what came later, after the wedding. We say more or less because as we grew up and found out more, in part because papá talked to us more openly, we realized we knew very little and few real facts, and what happened in those years was like the things we knew and imagined, but there was more, lots more to it.

Shihan was the last name of Mama Salima — papá's mother — and we all agreed that we would've liked to have had her cuddle and press us against her as kids because her chest seemed warm and cushiony. But she lived in Saginaw in the States and we in Mexico, and we saw her every six months or so and there was too little time during her visits to hug and cuddle us and when she did, it seemed to us that she never did it enough — we often think of her and miss her. Still we've seen photos and it's enough for us to know that she carried papá and squeezed and cuddled him against her warm and cushiony chest almost to the point of smothering him with so much love because Mama Salima loved him a lot for, among other reasons, he was her youngest son, and a mother is very fond of her youngest and grows very attached and doesn't want to let go of him and he of her, though papá did let go of his mother, only years later. Mama Salima sang cradle songs in Arabic and rocked him in her arms and loved him a lot.

Mama Salima loved papá and Uncle Gustav and Aunt Lou-ma from way back, from early in the century, and they were her family. Her husband was also family, but gradually we've learned that things between them weren't all that good and Mama Salima didn't really love her husband, papá's father, and that may be one reason why we know so little about Grandpa Rashid. We had already heard papá say one evening late at night that he himself was a bad father because he hadn't had a father from whom to learn to be good, and that's all we knew. Papá had somehow managed to work things out in his life without a father figure that mamá said was so important.

Poor Grandpa Rashid. When he came to the States full of hope, we're sure, he started off having to accept a change in name at Ellis Island, something we imagine he like anyone else didn't like. But the immigrants coming through Ellis Island were poor, and if they wanted to get ahead, they had to swallow their pride, yes, or give in, which is what Grandpa Rashid did. He gave up calling himself Rashid Nahum.

Papá remembers little about him, and to make things worse Mama Salima never kept or perhaps never had a picture of Grandpa Rashid, though there were cameras back then and people had already gotten into the habit of taking pictures and keeping photos of those they loved or had loved. But Mama Salima didn't have anything of Grandpa Rashid's, not even a picture, and so we couldn't form an idea of what he was like. We don't know if he was taller or stockier than Mama Salima, who was both. Grandpa Rashid was probably very short and skinny though we liked to think of him as being big and strong with a bushy mustache and lots of black hair when he stepped down on American soil on Ellis Island. From here and there we've been able to piece together that he was twenty years older than Mama Salima and she married him in the Hasrun mountains when she was fourteen. Their families married them off, that was the custom, and if she had been in love with him, perhaps she'd have painted an oil portrait of him on the boat that brought them — with brothers, sisters and all their furniture — for in those days the trip had to have been a long one and Mama Salima surely had many free hours on her hands. But if she had them — this was already at the turn of the century — she obviously spent her time reading, since it seems she had already picked up the habit. When Grandpa Rashid and Mama Salima, papá's parents, arrived at Ellis Island they were married and already probably drifting apart.

Lately we've begun imagining Grandpa's return to his homeland, with white hair and sunken cheeks, walking with a silver-handled cane not because he needed help walking but as a kind of weapon. We see him tall, thin, with the top buttons of his shirt open and a worn, loose coat. That's how we see him returning home, to the town where he was born. Sad or a bit angry. Maybe he had in mind to stay only a few months and then return to the States to rejoin Mama Salima and their three children — we're not sure, and we're also not sure whether he thought

51

that after a few months of having people call him by his full name, he could recover something that wasn't just strength and would permit him to return and face up to his adopted land, his business, his wife, and his children. Maybe that's what was really on his mind. But one day while he was there believing this or something else, he just up and died, and that's why he was buried there and never returned to the States or to his family and no one from his American family came to the burial and no one knows what name was put on the gravestone, if it was Rashid Nahum or the name they gave him at Ellis Island as a requirement for him to stay and to make it easier for others to address him and feel comfortable and closer to him. So that's how Grandpa Rashid stayed behind all alone and sad.

Apparently two of grandpa's brothers had emigrated to the States before or after him or at the same time on the same ship, but however it had been, they didn't get along and they never got together in the States. On the contrary, they grew further and further apart till they lost touch and forgot each other, and probably we've met uncles and cousins and maybe even nephews all over the world without knowing we were definitely related and not just realizing we look alike with a family air and a mysterious attraction connecting us. Mamá has told us that these uncles of papá went to live in Grand Rapids, but in all the trips we took with him in his Cadillac to the States, we always skirted Grand Rapids, though it would've been a shortcut, and we have no mental picture of the city just like we don't have one of Grandpa Rashid.

All we know is that when Grandpa Rashid left never to return — if he wrote letters in Arabic no one saved them — papá was at most seven and didn't remember anything or he hasn't told us the things he could remember, if he wanted to. So these unsubstantiated facts are all we really know about the first years of papá's life.

They lived in Manhattan, and papá was born there December 20, 1909, on the corner of Rector and Washington Streets. This was where Grandpa left from and never came back, and we're not quite sure if it was a tall building and on which floor the family lived.

Left a widow, Mama Salima for some reason decided to move to Michigan, to Flint, with all her things, even the Persian rug business that Grandpa Rashid had begun when he arrived. Rugs and knickknacks from the old country, and at one time even lamps, tables, and, we believe, pillows and mirrors and hookahs also: these were among the things that Grandpa imported from Lebanon to sell in the States. Once on her own, Mama Salima took over the business, and one day she decided to move it and the family to some other place and off they went. Maybe Mama Salima had read *Walden* by then and it had become her favorite book and she may have thought that the Lake State was closer to New England and Thoreau's world than a city with tall buildings and dark and narrow treeless and sunless streets like those of Manhattan.

They took all their things by train, and their arrival in Flint must've brought a certain degree of calm and peace to the family.

We know that Mama Salima was from a Maronite Christian family, and we suppose she became a Catholic because there were probably not enough Lebanese Maronites in Flint to carry on the traditions of her religion, and she began to wrap a rosary around both her fingers and the steering wheel of her old Chevrolet and from time to time would bump into someone in the right lane on the highway while she prayed. Mama Salima sang cradle songs in Arabic to her three children even if she probably hardly uttered a word to Grandpa Rashid, but to papá, Uncle Gustav and Aunt Lou-ma she spoke in Arabic which was the mother tongue of all of them.

And then papá began going to school just like his older siblings, and the three of them grew up speaking English and becoming Americans. Papá went to the same Catholic school as Uncle Gustav, but not Aunt Lou-ma, and there he became an altar boy and helped serve in the Mass just as we imagined his older brother did before him.

But papá's real life began on Saturdays when as a boy he was transformed into a true American, and in the mornings he delivered newspapers to his neighbors on a bike and in the afternoons spent the money he had collected buying books. Paper boy! was how papá announced himself, and when they opened the door he'd give them the paper.

We see it as something natural, natural for him to be or to have been a born reader, and we imagine him lying face down on a Persian rug with the rug pile tickling his thighs, though not to the point of laughter, and his legs crossed behind him. Once in a while he'd stretch a leg and the tip of a foot touches or

54

grazes a flower design on the rug and his face is in the crook of his hands and he is propped up on his elbows; papá is completely absorbed in reading one of the books he'd buy on Saturday afternoons after delivering the paper like all the other American boys like him did.

Papá bought his books at the drug store on the corner, but when he had reached the right age or met all the requirements, he took out a card from the local library and began to explore the shelves and check out books or read them in the library, at a table, though his feet couldn't touch the floor and he preferred to read at home, face down on a rug while Mama Salima cooked or smoked by the lit fireplace not thinking about anyone or missing anybody.

And naturally one book led papá to another, and one writer to another writer. As he was growing up, each year he read more and left behind children's books; he read different books which had started to arouse his interest so that by the time he was fifteen years old, he had read Bernard Shaw. In those first moments of his adolescence he acquired a liking for Shaw and his socialist ideas, and for one reason or another he even began to dream about one day going from where he now lived in Flint, Michigan, the Lake State, to Moscow.

So then one day he stopped serving Mass and attending church on Sundays, which surely shocked Mama Salima, Uncle Gustav and Aunt Lou-ma and got them thinking that he was not like them but still they would love him. Papá continued delivering newspapers, but he started getting other jobs that paid better so he could buy more books and read them face down on the rug.

By then Mama Salima had stopped working and Uncle Gustav and papá were the ones who began to support and take care of the family, working part-time while continuing to go to school and study and act like American teenagers, the children of immigrants, in the States.

Mama Salima had shut her business and now spent her time reading and smoking and also writing about the things she read or thought about for the Arab paper. She would hole up in the kitchen and pretend she lived in a wooden shack at the edge of a lake, or she'd walk around among the graves in the local cemetery, or take her old Chevrolet and slowly drive down the highway to buy fruits, vegetables and milk from her friends who owned working farms on the outskirts of town.

Time passed. Papá was growing up.

He went to Flint Junior College and continued his studies while at the same time he sold spinach wholesale and repaired telephone lines on the wooden poles all along Flint's main streets, obeying his superiors from the local Michigan Bell company who shouted instructions up to him from the sidewalk. If papá worked overtime, they'd pay him a little extra, and he could buy more books. In those days he didn't think he could fall from one of the poles or electrocute himself if he touched an exposed wire because he was young and he felt happy and had to support himself and the family and also buy books to read.

But then Uncle Gustav decided to attend college and study medicine and that's when papá began to work for the Standard Oil Company. He went from telephone cable lines to gasoline hoses, to washing the car windshields of his gas station customers on one corner of the city, to checking the air in tires, to adding oil and water for a few dollars more, on those afternoons and weekends when he didn't have classes at Flint Junior College and couldn't do what he liked most, which was, as it's always been, to read a book.

Back then he was surely not just a baseball fan but also played with his neighbors or with his Flint Junior College friends or those he worked with at the gasoline station who most probably were the same guys. He'd get together with them for a few hours at one place and later on the playing field, the drugstore, outside a movie house, or with a beer in hand sitting in a convertible belonging to one of papá's friends, with whom he made all kinds of different plans since he could talk to some of them about certain things and to others about other things and most probably he couldn't discuss with anyone the socialist ideas he had read about in Bernard Shaw's books and which he believed in, and so he and his buddies made plans, some of which seemed real and within reach, while others were unrealistic dreams like the one, in papá's case, of going to Moscow.

This was probably the day-to-day life in Flint in the year 1930, but for papá life was inside the books he checked out of libraries and which he read spread out in bed all through the night to the wee hours of the day, and this life was made up of history and literature.

And one day papá made up his mind and moved to New York to study journalism at some university. He left Flint behind him — Mama Salima, Uncle

Gustav, and Aunt Lou-ma, with their lives and their things were also left behind — so he could seek and find his own life down the road and not between the covers of the books he read but certainly based on them since they already formed part of papá's inner life.

By going to New York he was really going back to where he was born, and in college he made friends with people who would've been his childhood friends if Mama Salima, instead of closing the business and moving to Flint, had stayed with her children in New York. And like Grandpa Rashid, he probably imagined he would make friends in the place — Manhattan — where they had decided to settle down and live. With his new friends, who easily could have been his old friends, papá explored not only Central Park but also the old bookstores on Fourth Street. He moved from one attic room to another, first with one friend then another, always trying to find rooms close to Washington Square, the center of life or the place where people like them hung out, people who wanted to be writers, painters, musicians and the most popular actors, the kind of persons papá and his friends would get together with in the cafés to talk and pass the time.

And time passed.

One night a friend invited papá to a party at the Cape Cod house of Waldo Frank. In those days papá was a bit of a party-goer and he told his friend Yes I'll come, and he went. Waldo Frank was by then a well known writer whose books papá had read and admired, and it seemed an honor to be in his house. Papá told him so because at the time he wasn't given to his silent moods, and he gabbed and talked without even having had a drink to give him courage and make him forget his worries. Papá was happy that night for many reasons but also a little lost because by then he had given up on the idea of being a journalist and didn't really know what to do with his ideas, influenced by the socialist notions he had first read about in Bernard Shaw's books. He didn't exactly know what to do with his time, other than visit bookstores, libraries, park or café benches where he could sit and read in peace.

Among the guests at Waldo Frank's party was a young man like papá with whom he struck up a conversation over this or that till his new friend told him he was about to launch a new magazine in New York. He already had a name for it — *The Monthly Review* — and papá who was interested in the project and the magazine said so to his friend — in those days he liked to talk — who said to him Why don't you write for the magazine. They talked on and on finally deciding that papá could be a correspondent for the magazine; they discussed where he could go and from where he could send his articles and it would be, or could be, for example from Moscow. The pieces were coming together and papá's dreams and ideas were taking such solid form that he said Yes, why not, and he accepted without thinking twice about it and they shook hands and said It's a deal and so there, in Waldo Frank's house, the deal was closed.

But papá was quite young and not at all conventional, so instead of making a toast to his new boss, he climbed up a tree in Waldo Frank's yard as if it had been a Michigan Bell telephone pole and a co-worker had shouted to him from the sidewalk Go on up there and fix those cables. All around were the host's friends, contributors to *The New Yorker* and people like that — Mae West was also there — and papá looked down upon them from a branch and who knows what he was thinking, maybe not about anything, he just wanted to feel good and carefree, and he was happy when he noticed the others below starting to head toward the dining room — it was dinner time — and papá felt hungry up there and since he was young and impulsive, instead of climbing down the tree like a normal guest, he let himself go and yes, fell out of the tree on that dark Cape Cod night.

Dinner consisted of steamed clams, which he said were tasteless, and the party continued. At one point papá and *The Monthly Review* publisher asked Waldo Frank for a reference letter so papá could get a visa and leave as soon as possible for Moscow where Waldo Frank had already been.

Back then Constantin Umansky was the Soviet ambassador to the United States, and papá obtained a visa in the fall of 1934 through his intervention, and he left his West End and 85th Street apartment, left his belongings — mostly books — with various friends, packed his bags and set off. Once again he left Manhattan behind, and neither he nor Umansky knew then that one day they would again meet by chance in two other countries, something neither imagined, and so for the moment papá left for Moscow.

The fall of 1934 was not the best moment to arrive in Moscow, though it was for papá. From the start he lived like a Gypsy and put up with discomforts since he shared rooms with friends in apartments already occupied by large families. Papá arrived in Moscow without belongings but as time went on he accumulated things which, for the most part, consisted almost entirely of books. He bought many books of literature, history and biography and the most beautiful art books he would ever buy in his life: these were big volumes, with full-color plates and text in two, three, sometimes four languages. And it was in Moscow that papá first began to write.

He went to the theater, the movies, the ballet, and he would write on what he saw, the books he read, the people he met and the games he saw being played even if he didn't know the rules — like chess which he wrote on without really knowing what he was talking about. His friends were friends of Eisenstein, and his girlfriend at the time was Zenaida, Eisenstein's niece. One day she took papá to meet her uncle and he was introduced to him that day, and he saw and met him on other days as well. And one day he worked up the courage to ask Zenaida Eisenstein's uncle for an interview, but he refused and papá didn't take it badly; back then everything was permitted for this was a time in which he was still learning and this was part of his education. Zenaida gave papá one of her pencil drawings of a naked man, drawn from the back, sitting on a mountain top, possibly pointing to the horizon. She titled the drawing "The Precursor" and papá saved it.

But Zenaida wasn't papá's only friend in Moscow. Gerry — the Pole with the last name of Silverstein — was also his friend and together they traveled through the Soviet Union and went among other places to Leningrad and Bakú. They got along real well. Gerry studied medicine just like Uncle Gustav, and he was also polyglot: he spoke, read, and wrote in five or six languages, and papá really admired him and later, much later, to show how much he admired and cared for Gerry, he named one of us after him in his honor so as not to forget him and to have him present from morning till night for all the rest of the days of his life.

Moscow was really papá's university.

It was there he discovered culture, art, and history, and he did so many things for the first time in Moscow that sometimes it seems to us he was born and educated there, and it was the place where he became a man. In a way that's how it was and not just because that's how we saw it.

One night papá heard his first opera in Moscow and it was *Carmen*. There's nothing very musical about him, even if Mama Salima kept a book about opera on her night table. No music was ever played in papá's house, and yet he remembers feeling grateful his first opera was *Carmen* for he liked it a lot and maybe it played a kind of seminal role in his life, but for the moment it gave him so much aesthetic pleasure that he wrote a rave review and this pleased him. And even though he didn't know much about theater, and knew less about the theater he saw and wrote about in Moscow, he saw one play that impressed him as strongly as his first opera and which he also never forgot. The stage was right in the center of the auditorium and back then this was something new — anyway, it had a big impact on papá and he also remembers it with great delight. The playwright was there sitting in the audience and when he stood up, papá was impressed because the author was so incredibly tall and young, though not so incredibly young. Ohlohpkov was his name.

Time went by. Papá was living in Moscow and sending his articles to *The Monthly Review* in New York, which never sent him any payment. So meanwhile, papá submitted the same articles to the *Moscow Daily News*, which published each and every one of them in English, and to the magazine *International Review* which published excerpts in English and French. These two publications gave papá the pleasure of seeing his name in print for the first time, and he saw his name two or three times a week. He lived on what he made and later learned that a Polish magazine reprinted his *Moscow Daily News* articles, only they appeared in Polish translation in Warsaw; in that magazine papá published the longest article he ever wrote while in Moscow and which dealt with the Moscow subway. They featured the article in Poland and assigned two pages to it, with photos, and for this and other articles they sent him a fat envelope with twice the pay he had received for the same article in Moscow. He and Gerry celebrated with vodka — though we don't know if they also drank it down with red or black caviar.

But it wasn't the best moment to be living in Moscow.

The pleasure papá felt in seeing his name in the *Moscow Daily News* decreased when the authorities removed the publisher and put Borodin in his place. But to know what this meant, you have to know the details: Borodin had returned to Moscow in disgrace. He had been sent on a mission to meet with Chiang Kai-shek who had responded by kicking him out of

China, so the naming of Borodin as publisher was a kind of punishment, and this act made clear what the authorities thought about the *Moscow Daily News* where papá wrote. This event also merges with something of purely personal significance, which is that some years later papá and one of Chiang Kai-shek's generals played bridge at the same table in a country where they both were living — something neither would've imagined happening in their wildest dreams — and which brought papá double or triple the displeasure of being made aware again of Chiang Kai-shek in the person of one of his men.

And it also wasn't the best moment to be living in Moscow because around that time Kirov, a colleague of Stalin, had been assassinated, and the authorities kept a close watch on all foreigners in the Soviet Union. Papá was a foreigner and though he was happy to be there, he was being monitored one way or another. For example, some of his friends decided it was better not to be seen with a foreigner: they could no longer put him up in their rooms or share an apartment with him, and papá understood though he didn't want to move out because he was happy.

But then one day nine months had passed and papá's visa had expired. He insisted on staying despite this, so he ended up living in the country illegally for a month while he tried renewing his visa to stay in Moscow a bit longer.

Coincidentally, Umansky had come back to Moscow now as the Director of the Foreign Press and papá went to see him, but he wouldn't meet with him. Probably Umansky didn't even remember Waldo Frank or that he had recommended papá while he was still ambassador by intervening with the U.S. consulate to obtain a visa for papá. When this tactic failed, papá was ready to find another way, and he listened to everybody's suggestions, even the one to write directly to Stalin. Papá was young and impulsive and said Why not, and he wrote to Stalin and asked him, despite the circumstances and the moment in history, to intervene on his behalf so he could continue living out his dream of staying in Moscow. Someone had told papá If Stalin doesn't solve your problem, he'll at least answer your letter, but even so, Stalin never answered and of course didn't grant him an extension of his visa. But papá didn't lose hope because he was young and happy and he tried to find a solution through the *Moscow Daily News,* despite everything, but mainly because in the end that's where he worked and things were going well. So he went to see Borodin straight away despite everything. But Borodin told him There's nothing I can do to get them to renew your visa and also said he should continue writing and shouldn't stop turning in his articles despite it all. He went on to tell him that though he was the editor and in disgrace, and despite papá being a foreigner, he liked him very much. Papá wasn't offended that his boss couldn't help him: on the contrary, he remembers him as someone who tried to help him even if he walked around with a cane and things had gone so bad with Chiang Kai-shek.

Papá kept busy and time went by. Soon it was the summer of 1935 and the world kept spinning and so many things were happening. Despite it all papá was happy and wanted to stay on in Moscow even if his time was already up, and he was shifting from room to room living almost clandestinely at age 25 with a beard encircling his lips and covering his chin, a black, thick, curly beard not to be seen in mamá's oil painting of him which we saw hanging in their bedroom all through the years of our childhood.

A few days before papá had been in the Soviet Union for ten months, he went to a party. In those days he was a bit of a party-goer and dancer and while he was dancing, a tall and strong-looking man came halfway on to the dance floor. It was Paul Robeson and papá told him how much he admired him because in those days he was a talker and Robeson, for his part, praised his beard and the two Americans struck up a conversation right in the middle of the dance floor one night in Moscow. Papá told him what was going on regarding his expired visa and Robeson understood, and he suggested he not seek a renewal as a journalist because that caused problems but instead as a dance instructor because according to Robeson papá danced well, and they both started laughing. They never met each other again not there nor anywhere else.

In the middle of all this came the moment for papá to start dividing his belongings, just books really, and to pack his suitcase which he hoisted nearly empty onto his shoulder. He told his Moscow friends You take care of this and you of that because his plan was to return, and he didn't want to get rid of anything since he wanted all the things he had been collecting in Moscow though they were mostly books. At the train station he had to pay a 100-ruble fine for the expired visa and since papá assured the authorities he would be returning, they in turn assured him that the next time it would be a 1000-ruble fine, and papá laughed he was so happy even though he was also sad, for the moment had arrived to go and leave Moscow behind. He hardly had a thing in his small suitcase, and all he had were the "The Precursor" drawing Zenaida had given him and a box of Russian sweets, also from Zenaida. Though papá wanted to eat them, he thought it best to save them as a memento even if they'd turn hard and stale and gradually lose their color. And in his coat pocket he carried a couple of photos of himself which he had been obliged to take to meet the exit requirements.

It was the summer of 1935. Papá knew and felt that something was sweeping across Europe, and if he had to leave Moscow behind, he now wanted to go see with his very own eyes what was happening in the world: that would also be learning and living even if he had to leave behind his life in Moscow, which was where in a sense papá had been born.

On the train leaving Moscow and also all of the Soviet Union on its way to the rest of the world, papá had the luck and good fortune to be in the same compartment as Artur Rubinstein. Rubinstein had just finished a series of concerts throughout the Soviet Union and now was leaving for England, so he told papá. Rubinstein was a conversationalist and papá listened to him. In those days he too was something of a talker, and so he also told Rubinstein a few things, who in turn smiled, listened, and paid attention; the two of them struck up a conversation in the same compartment sitting face to face or next to each other while the Russian landscape rushed by the window and gradually stayed behind. And what did you do in Moscow? Rubinstein asked. Papá told him and he talked and talked maybe even stuttered a bit from having so much to tell because he wanted to, and he was so happy to have lived in Moscow and to have learned so much and to have begun to write. Rubinstein smiled and listened, and even though papá began to suspect that it would be wiser to talk less to better remember what Rubinstein might be able to tell him, he continued talking and then began to think that Rubinstein wanted to get away from him because it was a long trip, and perhaps he preferred to just look at the landscape of the country he was leaving behind and stop listening to the daydreams of a young, idealistic American who couldn't stop talking. At one point they had to switch trains at a particular station to continue their trip to the rest of Europe and while papá was looking for a compartment, Rubinstein caught up to him and told him they should sit together to continue conversing and papá felt doubly happy and said Yes, sure, my pleasure and so this way they arrived in Warsaw. Papá got off here and said goodbye to Rubinstein whom he would never see again but whom he had been lucky enough to meet. From the platform he saw his friend smiling at him for the last time in his life, and papá went off to the house of his friend Gerry the Pole, who had invited him and was waiting for him and who still hadn't changed his last name, Silverstein, to protect himself because it wasn't necessary yet. Papá stayed a month in Warsaw in the home of his friend's parents, and from there he went to Berlin to see for himself what was going on in Germany and in the world, and what he saw was the Nazis and their stormtroopers taking control of the streets and overrunning the city and country with their presence and then little by little all of Europe and the world, and the meaning of their intentions, which horrified papá, became clear and made him very sad. And from there he went to France and from there to England. Both France and England seemed to him to be asleep without realizing what was happening all around them and therefore hadn't become horrified yet. And from there papá went up to Finland, and from Finland he finally began his trek back home.

1935 was almost over and papá had been out of the States for over a year, and it was obviously hard for him to return and readjust with all that he carried within him, all he had left behind and all he knew was happening, such as Germany attempting to take over the world. It horrified papá and made him sad.

Immediately upon his return to New York he had one or two disappointments, but there were two that especially horrified and saddened him because he was young and many things still mattered to him. One had to do with the authorities of his country asking him What do you have in your trunk, and papá lowered it from his shoulders, opened it and told them Nothing but have a look for yourselves, and they looked and found a box of Russian sweets and asked What's this? They took the sweets away from him, and then and there in the Manhattan custom house he lost Zenaida's memento which he could've eaten piece by piece on the trip over. And the other disappointment was when papá asked about *The Monthly Review* and found out that it was not only not about to launch publication, but had yet to publish an issue and obviously had never printed a single article papá had written in Moscow and sent from there to Manhattan with the idea it would be published in the country and city of his birth. Right then and there papá regretted not having saved copies of the Soviet publications where they had certainly appeared, but it was too late to voice regrets, and the one sure thing was that his hands were empty.

That's not all because when he started asking and searching for the belongings he had left, with his friends, he found out that nothing was left and papá was upset though he had lost only books.

Between one thing and another a new phase started for papá who went on reading and marking time in Manhattan. Around this time he became friends with Ed Lending or maybe they were already friends from before. The thing was that one morning during those days they ran into each other and went to play tennis in Central Park. When they finished playing, one invited the other to a breakfast of fried eggs and bacon, but the other said No and then instead they went on walking and talking till suddenly Ed invited papá to become a member of his group, which was actually a Communist Party cell and papá said Sure. He joined and began to go with his friend Ed to all the meetings, and one night papá, Ed and a few other comrades went up on a ship anchored in New York harbor, supposedly to say goodbye to a friend, and they ended up burning the ship's flag which happened to be a Nazi flag.

The ship was called the Bremen or something, and papá remembered that the first shot was fired by someone who was disguised as a waiter but actually was a detective — it was later learned — who knew exactly what papá and his buddies were up to, and that's why he fired when one of them touched the flag and he pointed the gun at him. But papá, who was young and also impulsive, quickly snatched the gun out of the hand of the disguised detective and in one motion heaved it into the dark sea — planned and unplanned missions accomplished and just as the police arrived — and he and his friends escaped at full speed. Once they were safe, he realized there was blood all over his fist and yes, he was still bleeding. He remembers, whether or not anyone else does.

Yet papá and Ed's reason for attending the Communist Party cell meetings was to organize themselves to go fight in Spain. Little by little they got together and formed the Abraham Lincoln Brigade, and papá was part of it from the start along with Ed and also Jack — Jack Carpenter, already with his jaw like Popeye's — and Dell, another of Papá's friends who was tall and thin and ten years older than everyone else. There were others, many other comrades that already were or who eventually became friends of papá's and he of them and they were all together.

The Lincoln Brigade would form part of the International Brigades supporting the Spanish Republic against the rebellion of a soldier-traitor.

Back then papá and Ed shared an attic room. They were together all the time and talked on and on about the Party and what it had to offer them, and they talked about the same things with their comrades up there in the attic. Sometimes Alvah Bessie would join them and that's what they talked about; papá liked Alvah a lot, but Ed didn't like him as much.

Papá's Communist Party cell sent volunteers in groups of five by boat from New York to France, and papá once more had to leave his apartment toward the end of 1936 and set sail with his other comrades. Among them was a U.S. Army captain named Merriment; of this group he was the only one with military experience and on the passage over he taught them what he knew and all the men around him listened and tried to catch on so as not to start their mission knowing nothing. Another volunteer who made the trip from New York to France on the same ship as papá was a Mexican who told his travel buddies how many Fascists he was going to kill single-handedly because after all, that's why he was there and why he was part of the mission.

Yet when they arrived in Sète, France, they weren't allowed to get off the boat: the U.S. consul who received them said that the purpose of their trip was illegal — he knew about it and that's why he was there — and so he offered to pay for their trip back home, but not a single volunteer accepted and when they finally were allowed off the boat, the French authorities detained them and put them in jail. It seems that as groups of volunteers left the United States, *The New York Times* published lists with the names of those U.S. citizens who were going to Spain as members of the Abraham Lincoln Brigade so everyone knew who and why they were going. Papá's name as well as those of his friends appeared on one of these lists and as the authorities wanted to put a stop to this, papá, Captain Merriment, the Mexican and all those others who made it to Sète were detained and imprisoned.

A few months later they were finally set free.

Back then papá had already eaten artichokes for the first time and had concluded that it was too much work to end up eating only a small part of them.

The winter of 1936 was over and it was 1937. The ranks of volunteers continued swelling and some stayed behind, were scattered about, and completely forgot the reason why they had left the States in the first place, or said they hadn't forgotten, but would join the cause later, though a few had already decided not to. As soon as the Mexican volunteer was released from prison, he told his buddies he was going up to Paris for a few days and later would catch up with them. So the rest of the group set out for Perpignan where other groups of volunteers as well as contacts were gathered. They all waited there together for the Mexican and for others, but many of them had already begun to break away from the group and never managed to rejoin papá, his buddies and all the others in Perpignan.

In order to give the brigadiers their first taste of Spain, the contacts one night put them on a truck, which was supposed to transport oranges back from Perpignan to the Spanish side of the border, hiding them under a drop cloth. After a few hours of waiting and hiding, without the truck even moving, papá and his buddies began to eat the oranges and practice how to pronounce the fruit's name in the best Spanish accent with the "j" well stressed and varied by the different pronunciations the original language of each of them made. But before the sun came up, the drop cloth was taken off, and they climbed down from the truck; they were obliged to wait again for darkness to try a safer way to cross the border. During their stay in France, papá was appointed group leader because he among all of them was the only one who spoke some French, thanks to Mama Salima and her books. Also he was the one with the ambition to learn French though he didn't pronounce it all that well because he was young and many things didn't interest him while other things did.

It was the dead of winter. The scouts lined up the brigadiers to follow them as soon as it was dark. As the plan was to cross the Pyrenees on foot, the scouts handed out berets and espadrilles to the volunteers so they would all look alike — in one way at least — though this would in no way allow them to pass for a group of Spaniards or erase the most typical characteristics of the country from which each volunteer hailed. The trek was long and nothing easy, in darkness and in the dead of winter. A few of the men started lagging behind and had to be sent for while the others waited. Every hour or so everyone had to stop for roll call so nobody would get lost but also for them to rest for five minutes before going on to the Spanish border.

Papá was 27 years old and was the first volunteer, after the scout, to cross the border and step on Spanish soil. On the other hand, his friend Dell, who was ten years older, had to be sent for and waited for since he was lagging behind though, like papá and many of the others, he too wanted to keep on going and get there and not get lost or detached from the group and forget the mission. A scout went back to look for Dell, and papá saw them joining the rest of the group at the precise moment that a commander of the Spanish Loyalist Forces was welcoming them and expressing his gratitude to them on behalf of the Spanish Republic.

Then the training of the volunteers began, and the first order they received was to march for a stretch and for a set amount of time so their muscles wouldn't grow stiff; they were very tired from walking all night in the cold through French territory, but they all obeyed and complied with their first assignment on Spanish soil.

Papá was young and wanted to enlist in the Air Force and since in those days he spoke out, he told his Commander who told him that the Republic had few airplanes — they were old at that — and he was in no position to entrust even these planes to someone inexperienced; papá took it well because it was all part of his education, and he said to himself I don't blame him, and he showed he was prepared to serve the Commander and follow his orders. Papá, Dell, Ed, Jack and all their buddies, including Captain Merriment, received a month of infantry training after which papá was assigned to the Transportation Division for, among other reasons, he knew how to drive, and they now wanted him to take the wheel of an ambulance.

The first one papá drove in Spain had been donated to the International Brigades by Hollywood's actors and actresses. The first thing he did when he got it was to remove as best he could the red cross painted on the roof and also the identifying emblems and markings because he thought they made the ambulance an easy target for enemy flyers and he should cover them so the enemy would have one less target to attack.

A Brigade camp was in Almería on Spain's southeast coast and one of papá's assignments was to use the ambulance to carry food and equipment to

Madrid and to the southern front in addition to transporting the wounded. In less than two months and without having put on that many kilometers, the ambulance donated by Hollywood had been transformed into a jalopy with punctured tires and sounding like it was about to fall apart because the roads papá drove over were full of trash and all kinds of garbage or because the roads had been built by the brigadiers themselves and, given the situation, they hadn't done an ideal job, and so the ambulance bounced and rattled about. Papá too bounced along with it and was on the verge of falling apart at any moment just like the ambulance.

During the first day of the Ebro Offensive, for example, papá and his buddies transported 150 wounded of a 600-man battalion in less than 48 hours of nonstop driving. In just six days they had over 600 casualties and the ambulance papá drove was nonetheless an easy target for the Italian and German enemy pilots who didn't bother to cover their markings or try to pass for Spanish planes. So the war went on and papá's comrades went on dying and he went on transporting the wounded and food and equipment in his broken-down ambulance.

But this wasn't the only thing papá and his buddies did. In the middle of battle they found time to find one another or make new friends, and on one occasion with bullets flying a friend taught papá how to play chess and now he began to understand what the game was all about — the game he had written about in Moscow for the *Moscow Daily News* and of which a friend named Neider, an American like him, now began teaching him the first moves.

Then one day during those two years that papá fought as a member of the Fifth Regiment of the International Brigades' Abraham Lincoln Brigade in support of Spain's Loyalist Forces against a traitorous insurrection, he found his friend Gerry the Pole fighting like him in the middle of a pitched battle. Then on another occasion he had a similar chance encounter in the middle of the same war with his old friend Ed, whom he had not seen again since they had taken the boat to France with Captain Merriment and the others and made it to Spain. One night papá had driven two doctors to the Benicasim Hospital, and they had invited him to spend the night there and to continue on the following morning. Papá accepted their invitation for dinner and ate fried eggs — the first eggs he had eaten in a very long time — and they tasted unbelievably delicious. He thanked the medics he had driven and said good night to them and went to sit in the driver's seat of his ambulance and continued on his way deeper into the night, tired as he was and without knowing that probably that very night Lillian Hellman would visit the same hospital and he would forever lose the chance to meet her. But papá wasn't driving so well, and as he lurched half-asleep down the road on his way to Albacete trailing a truck he was unable to pass and which forced him to slam on the brakes every so often, he decided to pull over on the side and sleep for a while and ended up staying there and sleeping through the night. And the following morning, with apparently no set plan in mind, he decided not to go to Albacete where further instructions awaited him but instead he went to Murcia. Once there he went to the Brigade's main barracks and identified himself and that's how he met by pure chance his old friend Ed, and then the two of them hugged each other and didn't stop hugging though the battle raged on. Meeting Ed was a happy and unexpected event and one of them remembered the fried eggs and bacon breakfast the other had refused that morning while they walked across Central Park after playing tennis, which was before papá joined the Party cell that would eventually bring him to Spain. And there, in Spain, he and Ed regretted not having insisted and not having accepted and the two of them wished right out loud they'd have two fried eggs with bacon first chance they had, and papá didn't have the heart to tell his buddy that the night before two medics had invited him to eat — fried eggs to be precise — in the Benicasim Hospital, though without a side order of bacon.

But the war was uglier and sadder than this, and when papá began to see his friends being killed, he gradually became horrified and despondent; we believe this is when he also began to prefer silence to talking. Captain Merriment, whose name implies happiness and with whom papá had set sail from New York to Sète where they both had been imprisoned, was killed one day, and his was among the first deaths that papá felt personally, but then there were others, and the worst of them took place in Almería.

Papá was in charge of fifteen men and a convoy of trucks near Almería. They were about to head out with provisions toward Albacete and, as it was quiet, they decided to lunch on seafood before starting off on their trip. That's what they were doing when suddenly, before papá realized what was happening, bombs fell furiously upon them and a shell exploded where they were sitting, killing seven of his buddies and also wounding another five. All this while eating before heading out with provisions and equipment to one of their bases.

Four of the dead were Americans, one was French. Neider, who had taught papá to play chess, was among the dead Americans. Burgmaster, who like papá had been born in Manhattan, and Alexander were among the other dead.

While papá and the other two men who had survived the attack unscathed carried away the dead and wounded and tried to salvage and transport what was left of their equipment to the Brigade base in Albacete, they made out in the bay the five German battleships that had shelled them. On their way to the main barracks with the dead and injured, they found out that the attack had been in response to an air offensive by Republican forces, though everyone knew the Republicans didn't have the weapons for any such raid and had no idea what an anti-air defense system was. All the while the whole world slept around them — without knowing about this or anything else that happened or was happening in Spain — and allowed this to go on happening without doing a thing to stop it.

The large number of Americans in the Lincoln Brigade was gradually being reduced, the volunteer forces were fewer than before, and there were also fewer young Spaniards signing up. The time came when the Loyalist Forces decided that the remaining members of the International Brigades should return to their own countries so the Italian and German governments could withdraw their own men and equipment, and that's how the war began winding down.

But papá did not return to the States when the rest of his buddies did. He and another brigadier spent the last days of the war in a hospital fighting off malaria. 1939 was half over when he was finally discharged and returned to the States; by then the war had ended and the side on which papá and his buddies had fought had lost, even though it was the just side.

What papá faced upon his return to his native land after having fought for the Spanish Republic was that the U.S. authorities took away his passport and all his attempts to find work met with failure.

For a time he again lived like a Gypsy in Manhattan. He shifted from one attic room to the next, moving out when he ran out of excuses for why he couldn't pay the rent. That's what he was up to and what his life was about when the World's Fair opened in New York, and he was hired as Pavilion Director of the recently liberated Republic of Lebanon. The best thing about the job was that it let him meet mamá and that was no small matter.

From the time papá had left for Moscow in 1934 and returned to the States, he practically hadn't seen his family again. He even had them believing at one point that he was doing something different somewhere else like when he sent letters from Spain to Mama Salima through a friend who lived in England. He did this so no one would worry regarding his true whereabouts, but also because no one in the family shared his ideas.

But papá wasn't upset by all this. On the contrary, he enjoyed getting letters from Mama

Salima, where she'd write and tell him he had a second cousin living nearby and it wouldn't be so awful if he thought about her once in a while. So he had thought often about mamá, his second cousin, long before he got to know her, and this on the advice of his mother, our grandma. Papá thought about her and felt happy, and he thought about certain pleasant aspects of the war in which he had fought to feel pleasure and forget the unpleasant ones.

He'd lean back in his chair behind the display table in the Lebanese Pavilion at the New York World's Fair, and so as not to be sad, he'd remember, for example, the time he became a hero in the eyes of a comrade in Spain. Cigarettes were coveted by papá and his buddies in the war against the traitor, and they rolled their own though two thirds of the tobacco was actually the dust and dirt they found in their coat pockets. Once papá and a friend were resting on the side of the road when suddenly an enemy plane swooped down and attacked them. When the attack began, papá was only halfway done rolling a cigarette, and he and his buddy jumped into a trench. And what he did then — this made him a hero in his buddy's eyes — was that he didn't drop the tobacco for their last cigarette in the middle of what was going on.

And even if he smiled during the World's Fair as he remembered this to forget something else, that "something else" was there and made papá sad. From that moment on, he couldn't find a way to deal with all he felt and all he had gone through other than to become despondent and gradually grow more silent.

During the Fair he met and became friends with Yamil Barudi, the son of Lebanese immigrants like himself and the friend of many Saudi Arabians. On another occasion papá was with Elliot Paul and Carlos Quintanilla, and he also heard Will Durant declare at the Fair that Moscow was not going to fall and he was overcome with pride.

That's what he was up to, with little to do, when one day mamá came with her mother to the Lebanese Pavilion to meet and visit with him, her second cousin and the nephew once removed of grandma, mamá's mother. Mamá was traveling with her mother, and they had stopped off in Flint and had stayed there in Mama Salima's house. And on the mantelpiece, mamá had seen a photo of papá without a beard and had fallen in love with him though he was her second cousin, not a first, and Mama Salima had told them that he was her youngest son and was then at the Lebanese Pavilion and why didn't they visit him there. So mamá and her mother made another stop in Manhattan and yes, they went to meet and visit with papá at the World's Fair.

Papá was leaning back in his chair with his feet on his desk and his hands locked behind his neck, sometimes recalling the happy parts of the war in which he had fought, gone hungry and been on the losing side and at other times remembering the sad parts he wanted to forget. It was then that he saw mamá and her mother standing at the entrance to the Lebanese Pavilion.

Oh, so it's you, he said to mamá knowing exactly who she was. She nodded, and they fell in love, though mamá was in love with him even before meeting him since she had seen the photo of him without a beard and thought It's him.

But more than two years went by from that first encounter till the time of mamá and papá's three weddings.

During that time they wrote letters to each other and mamá would come and visit papá, her second cousin, who was now her fiancé, and they traveled across the United States always accompanied by grandma, mamá's mother, and sometimes they stayed with Mama Salima who had already moved to Saginaw into the house in the middle of a forest where the railroad tracks and even the train went by.

When the World's Fair ended, papá managed to land a job with the George A. Fuller Company, a huge construction firm with offices on the 18th floor of the Fuller Building on 57th Street and Madison Avenue. By then it was 1943 and papá resigned from this job so he could be drafted into the U.S. armed forces when the States finally decided to enter World War II on the only side that was right.

Papá did his basic training in Miami where he became friends with Marsh Holleb and from there he was sent to the army's Central State College in Edmond, Oklahoma. He was there with six hundred other soldiers and he learned, among other things, how to type well — not with just two fingers as he had done in Moscow. He had such a hard time of it that all his buddies congratulated him and applauded on the day he passed the exam by typing at a speed of thirty words per minute. But he didn't do so well on the final test: only eight out of the 600 were going to be chosen as officers and though he managed to make the final eight, he was eventually eliminated, unlike Marsh who, as soon as he passed, began to move up in rank.

It seems that during the personal interview papá's attitude and answers did not satisfy the officers who sat on the other side of the table from where he stood at attention in a uniform that was too small and made him uncomfortable.

Ten officers faced him, some of whom seemed fairly decent but the rest had the kind of sadistic attitude one tends to associate with the career officers of all armies. And the one with the worst attitude interviewed papá.

He began by reading in front of the others the army's file on papá, emphasizing two parts: that from 1934 to 1935 he had studied in Moscow's Lenin School of Journalism, and that from 1936 to 1939 he had been a member of the Abraham Lincoln Brigade fighting in Spain. Papá didn't deny any of this or seem at all ruffled by it and the officer went on to ask him if he felt smart enough to aspire to be an officer in the United States Army, in "intelligence" no less, he could surely define the term in ten words.

Papá replied that he could define it in five words: "Gather, select and disseminate information."

Because of this answer, though they did let him join the Army just a few days before they ended the sign-ups, they sent him to Tinker Field, a boot camp in Oklahoma City, which was where they kept him frozen for two years till he decided to quit. But papá wasn't upset by this because he was still young and believed it was all part of his education.

The letters he wrote to mamá had to be approved by a censor before she could receive them and the censor would stamp a number on the envelope, a number she knew by heart because he always stamped the same one. And the letters she sent to papá were also read by a censor before he got them and the number was the same one stamped on his letters to her, so they both knew that the censor followed the course of their lovemaking but they didn't care and luckily the censor let them continue.

One of those days in September of 1943 papá took a long weekend and went to see her in Saginaw where she was staying with her mother in Mama Salima's house, this after they had written so many letters back and forth from one side of the U.S. border to the other, in Mexico where mamá lived. And one of those mornings papá and mamá took advantage of the situation and without telling anyone they secretly went to city hall. A guard and a secretary about to retire were the witnesses to their marriage. Their thinking was more or less correct: the only way papá could've obtained the army's permission to go and marry mamá in Mexico was by proving he was already married to her under U.S. law. But no matter how good their logic was in secretly marrying in Saginaw, it set off quite a family scandal since the following morning an announcement appeared in the local paper. A helpful neighbor brought the news to the two cousins, now in-laws, while they ate breakfast and talked in Arabic around the table.

As it was, and in light of the fact that the U.S. authorities hadn't returned papá's passport to him, he crossed the border with an ID card and a seven-day pass and on November 8, 1943, he married mamá two more times: in a civil ceremony to meet the requirements of Mexican law and in a religious one by walking down the center aisle of a church in

Mexico City dressed as a buck private of the U.S. Army while he hummed to himself. She walked down the aisle, wearing a smile, which was the refrain of a song popular during those October days when the whole world was at war. The lyrics gave him the image of a bride who walked down the center aisle wearing a smile but nothing else.

They spent their honeymoon in Cuernavaca, and before the seven days were up, the U.S. Embassy found papá and relayed the order that he had to return to Tinker Field as soon as possible. Mamá and papá had to stop whatever they were doing to pack up and fly back to the Midwest where they set up house as newlyweds in Oklahoma City.

There papá taught mamá how to cook, and while she learned, they ate fried eggs with bacon and boiled potatoes for two months till she grew bold enough to ask the employees at the grocery store how to cook spinach, and they answered her Like everyone else does. How do you cook it? and she said to them I asked you first, and then they told her how. Gradually she learned and during her free time she began working on an oil painting of papá without a beard which she painted completely from memory from being so in love with him.

The Army assigned papá to the Transportation and Rails Office but he had nothing to do; they wouldn't even let him do office work like typewriting letters now that he knew how to type professionally, and that's when from doing absolutely nothing, he began to develop a passion for mystery novels. Reading this kind of book is how he secretly passed his working hours since he wasn't allowed to work.

That's when he met Herb Federbush.

Papá revealed to mamá his hunch that the army had a spy watching him. Naturally she blamed it on the books she herself had also given him to read in their newlyweds' house. She told him It can't be true, till the afternoon when he invited her for ice cream in the center of town and she herself saw the man papá had described to her following them from the moment they left the house. He sat down at a nearby table at the ice cream parlor and ordered the same ice cream combination as they — a scoop of vanilla and one of coffee in a cone with melted chocolate and crushed almonds on top.

That's how it was and how things went.

The Army had a spy watching papá. He did his work spying on him for several months till one day papá invited him for a cup of coffee, since he wasn't bothered by all this. The man accepted and they became friends, and he told papá My name is Herb Federbush, and papá and Herb shook hands and struck up a conversation across the table with a cup of coffee between them. Herb didn't waste any time in telling papá that, yes, he was spying on him. Herb was supposed to report where papá went and with whom he spoke and what he read and also to whom he wrote and from where and from whom he received letters and of course what these letters contained or were about. But Herb either quit or his superiors for one reason or another relieved him of his assignment. Still, Herb continued to follow papá but this time like a friend, and he liked papá so much he wrote an article about him in the *Tinker Tailspin*, which was the camp newspaper, and which revealed how much he admired papá. Mamá and papá were also very fond of him and showed it, and when they decided to leave the army, the camp, and Oklahoma City, they left their newlyweds' house to Herb, Herb Federbush, the man who spied on papá.

Mamá, and what was already formed of the oldest of us in her womb, left Oklahoma before papá and flew to Mexico City, sharing the same airplane seat on a flight that was oh so long. Papá stayed behind to quit the army which never promoted him and which had frozen him and never given him a chance to fight with the Allies, and once again against the Fascists. On the contrary: they blocked him from doing it and always made him feel that because of his past he would never go very far or go anywhere at all. They didn't even want to profit from papá's spirit, which was good and on the right side, nor from what he knew and could do from typing well on a typewriter, to speaking a bit of French, a bit of Arabic, and a bit of Spanish, which should have earned him a trip to Africa or even to Londonderry where he wanted and requested to go, because at that time, though he spoke less than before, he still spoke more than he did later.

And so after he resigned, he bought an old used Ford and filled it up with books and pots and Persian rugs. He tied down the suitcases real well on top of the car and covered them with a green cloth that was part of the gear of an ex-buck private in the U.S. Army. He sat behind the wheel and took the highway going south; with his left elbow sticking out of the window, he headed toward the border, toward the new life he was about to begin, even if he had no passport and his pants pockets were empty. That's how he drew away from his country as well as from its landscape, and its customs and gadgets stayed behind. Papá was on his way and looked straight ahead from behind the windshield and who knows what he hummed to himself during that time because papá has never been very musical.

This was what papá's life had been like before, and this was the moment when his former life was going to come to an end so his life to come could begin and go on as far as it could. Papá drove down the main highways, always heading south, and on the Mexican side of the border people and things and situations waited for him as they would happen, most of which he never imagined happening while he drove and left his country behind.

Mamá's father had sent an official named Palazuelos to help papá cross the border. Mr. Palazuelos was waiting for him, shook his hand and welcomed him to Mexican territory at the same time the customs and immigration authorities came up to welcome him, though instead of offering him their hand, they slit open the green cover which he had put over the suitcases on top of the old used Ford. They then opened the suitcases and took everything out, but there were only books and pots and Persian rugs. They went through it all and put it back into the trunk only now papá was unable to close the suitcases and that's how he entered the country and how he made it to Mexico City with the cover torn and his books and things all over the place.

3

The Appointment and the Bridge

"The lousy articles I wrote! I'd like to read them again! I'll write them again, someday."
Emile Jacobs

When Mama Salima died, we were all sitting around the table drinking coffee, grown-ups and kids, waiting for either papá or mamá to tell us You're excused. Our nanny appeared at the door and with an anxious, faltering voice said to mamá that someone was calling papá long distance. He went to the telephone, and we saw him pick up the receiver and say to Aunt Lou-ma and Uncle Gustav You don't say and I'll be coming and he lowered his head and sobbed. This was the first time we had seen him like this though we had seen him sad before and then he packed just one shirt and a change of underwear into a small black suitcase. He went to the airport all by himself wearing his dark suit and he told mamá before leaving Be back soon and he gave her a kiss and he avoided our eyes and we didn't know what to do or what to say to him. He came back a few days later, and he was still sad though he no longer cried, and we recalled, alone among ourselves, the last time we had seen Mama Salima who hardly even recognized us. We'd walk by her and her eyes barely focused on us since she stared blindly into the distance. She'd be smoking and the smoke enveloped her face, and we assumed that that was why her vision had clouded up and she said nothing, but we didn't know how to express our condolences to papá, and all we did was to wait for time to pass and, yes, it passed.

By then papá had already sold the hotel and spent more time than ever reading. Mamá began to worry about this and when she spoke on the phone to her friends, partly in French and partly in English and half in Arabic, she told them I'm worried, and we understood she was referring to the fact that papá spent the whole day in the house and that gradually he stopped answering his letters, and he already had stopped hosting his New Year's Eve party in that first year without a hotel during which he was turning into a retiree.

That's why mamá thought it would be a good idea to cheer him up, so for his 50th birthday she gave him a gold watch — from her and all of us — with our names engraved on the back. Papá's first reaction was not to accept the gift even before opening it, and he even got up angrily from the table and threw down his napkin and didn't finish his dinner. Mamá had to wait an entire day for him to finally say Okay, yes, he would accept what we all had gotten him, and he put on the watch and never took it off again, and every once in a while we heard him say This is my treasure, and smile. It was his only treasure because by then he had given up the Cadillac, and he never had and didn't have fine clothes. In terms of books, only he knew their true value, and it was clear that he would never say in front of us that books were his treasure because he imagined we wouldn't have understood him, and he was probably right.

Then, for who knows what reasons, because things were going well, or at least we hadn't realized that they weren't going well since we were busy studying and busy doing more or less what we had done till that moment, except perhaps traveling, and then some of us had already begun to work, so no one noticed but we had begun running short of money at home. We all liked buying what we wanted to buy, because in those days we never desired anything that we couldn't afford. And since we weren't short of food or wood for the fireplace, we couldn't really know if there was something wrong in papá's accounts because even if he talked to us more now than ever before, household finances were not discussed with any of us and mamá took care of things in such a way that none of us, neither of her parents, or the rest of the family, could notice that something was wrong and that we were beginning to run short of something.

What happened is that one day papá began to invite a Spanish refugee named Paquito to the house and the two of them locked themselves up to talk, and soon they started a business and they became partners. Their business was to import or export cigars, and Paquito smoked cigars and though papá didn't, it seemed as if some serenity had come back to his face and perhaps he even regained a bit of his happiness. The house, as if by magic, seemed to brighten, and it appeared as if everything that had been quietly still had suddenly come to life. We again began hearing conversations and even laughter in the house, and the doors didn't only close but actually opened, and papá and Paquito began to prosper, and though we never had another Cadillac again, papá managed to buy a few lots in Florida. Since he was the only one in the firm who spoke English, he was the one who took the business trips to New York. He visited Dunhill's on Fifth Avenue, and he went to

London and to Canada, and even mamá's parents became happy for him and their daughter, and for a moment it seemed as if the bad times had finally come to an end and fortunately were a thing of the past.

We all liked Paquito, especially the females among us, because he'd invite us to the bullfights, though we didn't enjoy them, but we were lucky enough to see El Cordobés. He also took us to the best restaurants, and though we didn't even know what to order, we felt so grown-up because we could put on make-up and we had to behave as if we were adults. Paquito would laugh and wouldn't take his cigar from between his lips, not even to drop the ashes that stayed suspended in the air till they fell down on their own, though rarely into an ashtray.

Paquito's suits were always too big for him, and though he wasn't that handsome, he was always inviting a woman — not just mamá or the females among us — to the bullfights or to a restaurant or to the theater, though it was true that he never took his own wife anywhere. One night one of us saw Paquito in the theater with one of his girlfriends, and she caught a good glimpse of the woman so she could tell the rest of us what the woman was like and what impression she had made. And she told us that the woman was very pretty and appeared to be a Gypsy or a dancer and even if she weren't so young, she could've danced even nude in front of a mirror till Paquito would tell her Stop and come over here and then she wouldn't even care if she'd end up smudging Paquito's shirt collar with the red paint of her thick lips, which seemed to be always wet or glowing, though her hair glowed even more, and even if it were up in a bun, it gave the impression of being loose and swaying limpidly to and fro and making the sound that silk makes when it's stroked with the tips of the fingers.

Papá liked Paquito a lot, and one day he told him that one of us females had been invited to a fancy dinner and didn't have anyone to go with. Paquito told him that he knew who could go with her, and what he did was telephone a son of the ambassador of the Spanish Republic in Exile living in Mexico and asked him to take our sister to the party. He took her and they became friends, and then the ambassador and his wife became friends of papá and mamá. Paquito smiled, with a cigar in his mouth, happy to have connected papá's present to his past; papá, mamá and the rest of us began going to the Embassy without fail at least once a year on April 14th to celebrate the Republic, and papá stood out among the guests, at least to us who saw him happy to be among the refugees and the other guests, which sometimes included Siqueiros and people like that with whom papá could converse, not only remember and make toasts with.

But one day Paquito vanished, and neither his wife nor the Embassy nor the police nor papá ever heard from him again, and no one knew if he had died or if he had gone to Spain or some other place. And naturally the cigar business collapsed and papá and the house grew dark once more. Mamá began to worry and call her friends and tell them that she didn't know what else to do but to save and try to make do once again without any income and with papá once more spending the whole day sitting in his chair with a book in his hands and submerged once again in his retirement which consisted of being ever more silent.

After he had returned from Mama Salima's funeral, one of us one day heard him briefly telling mamá that Aunt Lou-ma and Uncle Gustav hadn't wanted to give him anything that Mama Salima had left behind and that he had only asked to keep her books but they had said No. They then scolded him for having left the States as if he had done this just now and as if he didn't have or wouldn't have had the right to go any place wherever and whenever he wanted, but that's the way it was and they said No. And despite it all, Aunt Lou-ma acted as if nothing had happened since she went on calling him every year on his birthday, but it seemed as if he had had a fight with Uncle Gustav and papá didn't want anything to do with him. We imagined that Uncle Gustav also didn't want to have anything to do with papá, his youngest brother. And worse, papá began to take on the look of an orphan or of someone in exile or of a man without family or country, and he sank into his readings and said nothing to anyone.

Another day, also at dinner time, one of us came home with a record and put it on. Though papá had no interest in music, the second he heard the opening words of the first song, he was so disturbed right in front of all of us that we had to shut the record player off. The record had Spanish Civil War songs and had been given to one of us by a friend who had said Your father's going to like this one. He may have liked it, but his shoulders heaved up and down and he lowered his head to his chest and sobbed. When mamá saw him like this, she also sobbed, and we didn't know what to do, and the only thing we wanted was for something to come along and put an end to papá's sadness.

We don't know how it happened, but one day a very elegant gentleman named Del Río, with a very well-trimmed grey mustache and a well-cut suit, came to the house. One way or another he and papá planned or hatched a business and they became partners. Gradually the shadow that covered the house as well as papá's somber mood began to lift, and mamá started smiling again and baking almond cookies. And though we never again celebrated New Year's Eve at home, Papá's partner Del Río would give mamá a box of giant shrimp and each year she prepared them differently, following new recipes. There was no one at home who didn't smile, least of all papá, who smiled the most though he didn't stop reading and buying books or checking them out of the library. He subscribed to magazines from the U.S., not only news but also business magazines which we all thought were boring but which seemed to interest him. The business with Del Río prospered, and when it was about to come to an end, the two partners — each wary of the other — made separate arrangements with clients not to be left with nothing, and that's how papá hooked up with an English-Canadian company which was about to go bankrupt. But papá kept it from going broke and actually got it to grow and instead of eating lunch at home every day, he ate with one or two of his employees. His employees were fond of him and gave him gifts like a luxury English edition of *Don Quixote* with the text in gold leaf and illustrations by Doré because they knew he had a soft spot for Spain. Though he never told them exactly why he had that soft spot, he was very moved by the book and placed it in a special book shelf in the living room. Mamá was also happy and once again she stopped worrying, after having worried a lot about his retirement and the way he cut himself off every time he retired.

But some fifteen years had already gone by since papá had sold the hotel, and in any case his sixty-fifth birthday was approaching and for some reason or another the company told him That's it. Papá couldn't do anything about it, and he was left without a pension, without severance pay or anything, just a suit because they decided to sue him. Papá had to hire lawyers, and this, together with his usual retirement habits, led him to pull his name from the telephone directory. Though he no longer answered letters or phone calls now, he had us tell whoever called him that he was dead. We, out of pure superstition, didn't obey him but instead said He doesn't live here anymore, and if they asked us Where does he live now? we'd answer that we didn't know.

Then one day while we were sitting around the table, our nanny came up and told mamá once again that someone was calling papá long distance. We saw him answer the call, and after hanging up once more, he went to his closet and took out a shirt and a change of underwear and packed them into a small black suitcase. We heard him telling mamá that Uncle Gustav was gravely ill in the hospital and that he was going to see him and off he went. Then later, much much later, we found out that papá had managed to see his older brother for a little while the very evening before he died and that fortunately they had shaken hands and made peace. They also cried before saying goodbye when a nurse told papá You have to go. He had to interrupt his visit without having had more than enough time to say to Uncle Gustav I love you and Uncle Gustav, in turn, also had just enough time to say the same thing to papá while he lay in pain in a hospital bed.

And during those days for several reasons papá and mamá had to move out of their house and into mamá's mother's house. By then all of us had already left home, each to a different place, and some of us had even left the country. So though the house was, for this reason alone, no longer the right house for papá and mamá, it continued to be their home, and it was very difficult for them to leave it. It was so difficult that they even left a few things in several closets so they'd have to return for them. But they never returned so that they would always have to think of returning for them one day.

But this happened because time passed and had passed and there was nothing else to be done. Then papá and mamá got used to the new house, and mamá came and went and made it also into her house but papá couldn't: he kept to himself in his room and wouldn't come out and his room became practically his whole house.

From time to time one of us had an idea which we proposed to papá so that he wouldn't sink into total retirement. Though he listened to what we had to say, that was it, and gradually we decided to leave him in peace. One idea was for him to open a bookstore because mamá was growing more and more concerned that all he did was read. We also suggested that if he didn't want to open a bookstore, what about a travel agency, but his answer was no, that bookstores made no money and that there were already too many travel agencies. One of us even suggested that he then write his life story, but he also said no to this though he sobbed while he said it. We all began to feel little by little that there was nothing we could do. We each decided to leave him alone in peace, reading in his old chair by a large window through which the sunlight streamed all day and all afternoon and through which he could see the trees in the garden and, beyond a low wall, a bridge.

The bridge papá saw from his window was simply made of stone, and it went up and down between two thick railings that were as old as the rest of the bridge; here, in the late afternoons, lovers would sit and hug each other for a while, though no river ran under it, just earth and pasture and the garbage mixed in with the piles of dead leaves.

When we visit papá in his room, we sometimes see him raise his eyes from the book he's reading and gaze at the bridge. He recites to us all a quote he recalls from when they moved here and he saw the bridge: The law in its infinite justice prohibits both rich and poor from sleeping under bridges and begging for alms on the streets, and he asks us if we've heard the quote before and to find out the author of it, because he's forgotten. Then he smiles and asks us See if you can guess whether it's the rich or the poor who choose to sleep under a bridge and beg for alms and before we can answer him, he's back to his reading which could be James Thurber's *The Years With Ross* or a rereading of Gibbon's *The Decline and Fall of the Roman Empire.*

But papá doesn't spend his whole day sitting and reading. He also listens to a U.S. radio station or television channel for the latest news reports and he also watches The World Series and the tennis championships on TV. He even makes bets with some of us or with our children or nephews and he cheers up as he watches, even if his team or player loses. Papá always bets on the baseball team which has the largest number of black players, whether from the States or Latin America, and on the tennis players from socialist countries. But when the winner is the typical North American youngster, he gets angry, even shouts, and it's not because he's lost the bet. Those of us watching the game with papá are upset by his behavior while the others point out to us that his attitude is consistent with the way he's lived his life, at least his earlier life, and that his attitude is in fact amusing.

But all this still worries mamá, and she tells papá that he should at least do some exercise and not spend the whole day sitting. So then for a while he'll take the dog out for a morning walk, more to please mamá than anything else but also because he's put on weight and no matter how many diets he goes on, he doesn't shed pounds, and this worries him.

There are many things that worry papá.

Aunt Lou-ma, for example. One day he went to visit her and when he came back he told us — rather he told mamá and one of us somehow heard about it — that she can hardly see and she confused him with Uncle Gustav and not once did she call him by name. And papá also worries about not having an income and having to live off of savings and that this money buys less each day. This also worries mamá, but so as not to worry him she somehow makes do, but each time she makes do with less, and we don't know exactly what to do because there's nothing we can do no matter how much we try.

Under the glass on his night table papá keeps a newspaper article which we see when we visit him. It's a cartoon of the Mexican President on the day he takes power. In the first frame he is a thin and simple man entering a door marked President of the Country and in the second frame he is leaving six years later when his term is over, and he's a very fat man with a very heavy bag on his shoulders which contains thousands and thousands of gold coins.

At one point papá let us pay his way to New York. He went alone, stayed there for more than a week and when he got back, he told mamá that he hadn't looked up any of his old friends for fear of finding out that they had died. Instead he looked for the old bookstores he used to visit on Fourth Street when he was a young man but he didn't find any. He also told her that everything seemed to have changed a lot and that one day he had tripped and fallen on the subway steps and that no one had come to help him up. Then on two or three occasions he had been able to help people who had asked him how to get to a particular place, and this had made him happy, not only because he had remembered but also because he had given them the impression that he had been living in New York for many years. And he also told mamá I don't know where I would like to live, but certainly not in Manhattan: that he was sure of, though he had been born and had spent his youth in Manhattan and he had been young and happy there.

And for similar reasons he no longer subscribed to nor bought *The New Yorker* because, among other reasons, all the contributors he had read as a young man had died, and the new ones weren't any good, and in any case he had absolutely no interest in reading them.

It was around this time that one of us began having dreams about going to New York. Each time he tried to make it to St. Patrick's Cathedral, something happened which kept him from reaching it, or if he got there the door was shut. He could never get in, and he told the dream to the rest of us and all of us felt that it was an omen, a sad one at that, because it showed that something one of us wanted and which was what all of us wanted and want, we wouldn't get. It was worse than that because it had to do with papá, so that like, when as children we wanted to sing to him Papá we miss you, Papá we love you, and Papá we need you, and even though by doing it we sounded like children, we all knew and knew it deep down inside, that when we talk about papá we always sound like this because this brings us a little closer to him, which is where all of us want to be since he has a lot to do with the time before, which is the time we were all happy. At this very moment we also wanted to sing to him, but something held us back, and all of us kept locked inside that which we wanted and which involved papá.

During this whole period mamá was the one who worried most, and we see her planning activities to amuse papá but which he doesn't really like because the one thing he really likes to do is read in peace. He's never bored by this — we're not sure if he's sad — though it appears he is and this seems to be true. Perhaps he hasn't forgotten any of the things he thought he would forget. That may be it. Mamá has tried to revive papá's bridge games, but she's had to face the fact that most of the players have died or moved away or, like papá, they'll do anything but revive any game — bridge or otherwise — because they are where they are and the only thing they want is to be left in peace.

But one time papá gave in to one of mamá's ploys to rescue him from his full retirement, and he agreed to call one of his old friends long distance who lived in Mexico and was not among those who had returned to his country. He was from Italy, Turin was the city where he was born, but when he became widowed, he left his house in Mexico City and moved to Cuernavaca which was precisely where papá and mamá had spent their honeymoon some forty years earlier. Papá called and mamá heard him talking, even laughing with his friend, and she heard him promise that one of these days he would go visit him. He would even spend one or two nights with him because they really had much to talk about, and if everything worked out, perhaps they could even bring together a few old friends, revive the teams and play bridge like in the good old days. Why not? And she heard him sound truly animated, and she thought to herself that finally one of her attempts to rescue papá had led to something good, but then she heard him hang up and saw him go, confused as a little boy into his bedroom, despite his seventy-odd years of age.

He simply dropped into his chair. Mamá let him be, and the two of them stayed by themselves in the room that no longer had the oil painting she had painted of him when they were newlyweds and he was a buck private in the U.S. Army and mamá was just learning to cook and be a wife and a homemaker and she still had many free hours during the day and she was so in love with him she painted papá completely from memory. When papá had calmed down there next to the window, from which he could clearly see the old stone bridge, mamá knelt by his feet, hugged his legs — according to the one of us who was watching from the other side of the half-opened door — and asked What's wrong, while she looked at him and tried to calm him. He's my only friend and I hardly get a chance to see him, he answered, and he wept till he calmed down while the afternoon passed and darkness could be seen through the window.

To keep him busy, mamá decided that he should be in charge of certain household chores like ordering and receiving the gas and paying the bills at the bank every one or two months — she would tell him which had to be paid when. She suggested that he walk there, though early each morning he took a stroll because it was good for him to exercise. Papá obeyed her and every evening he would put his papers in order and would take the paid stamped bills and file them away. Yes, it seemed as if he was enjoying his retirement a little. He realized that these were worthwhile tasks when he sat down to read or listen to or see the news and hear the commentaries, for papá kept abreast of what was going on in the world although in his own personal life he continued his retirement.

Every once in a while he would hear from certain old friends living in the States. Mamá was the one who answered the letters or post cards sent, for example, from China, like the one from his old war buddy Marsh, who was now a successful lawyer in

Chicago and who, despite everything, remained a loyal friend to papá, or from Israel from where before he would've truly enjoyed getting something but which now made him feel a mixture of sadness, confusion, even anger. When one of those things happened which happened in the world more and more often he said that Israel like the United States had become a terrorist state despite everything, incredible as it seemed. It hurt papá — it wasn't necessary to say why — but a friend would write to him from the States and tell him he just had another grandchild and mamá would answer that they just had another one also. They compared and kept count, and papá and mamá would lower their heads because in the world's eyes they were also losing since they were the only ones to have just five grandchildren. Yes, they would've loved to tell their old friends they had many many more and that all their children were doing well and were successful and didn't suffer or hadn't yet suffered, but they couldn't write this to anyone because it wasn't true, and this made papá and mamá very sad.

At one point one of us heard mamá ask him which had been the happiest time in his life and he'd answered When the children were young, which was like saying when the whole family lived together in the other house, though from the time we were very young, the females among us really lived in mama's parents' house in the very room where papá and mamá now live and which, for all practical purposes, is now his entire house.

Every once in a while Jack, papá's old friend, the one with the Popeye-like jaw, would come to Mexico. In one of his last visits, because he too vanished, he insisted that they go together to visit an old member of the Lincoln Brigade living in Mexico. Papá didn't know him, but Jack did, since he kept track of all the members he could and tried to organize reunions or at least let them all know what each of them was doing. Papá agreed to see him and they went to his house. The man was a musician named Conlon Nancarrow, who lived as isolated as papá but who played music which drifted from the house where he lived closed up and traveled all the way to New York where it was being heard and listened to. Jack and papá went to Conlon's house one Saturday morning and they saw the *pianolas* he used for composing his music. They talked about the Spanish Civil War, according to what Jack told mamá when they got back, but they didn't want to hear Conlon's music for among other reasons papá isn't that interested in music. Conlon wasn't offended but once Jack returned to the States, papá didn't go visit Conlon and Conlon didn't come and visit him. Both continued secluded in their own retirement, though Conlon's traveled through walls and began gaining recognition and even respect while nothing happened with papá's because he wouldn't answer letters or phone calls and he really wasn't the least bit interested in unions or reunions or so it seemed on the surface. We didn't know what went on inside of him and what these reunions really meant to him or did for him and how they were affecting him more each time.

Then one day even Jack stopped visiting and writing to papá and the letters that mamá mailed to Jack's house came back unopened. Papá and mamá guessed that Jack had died, and mamá chose not to talk about it and not sadden papá or make him sadder than he actually was. Apparently Jack had had a son, but he never got in touch with either papá or mamá, and she wasn't at all sure that his son actually existed since neither of them had ever met him, and Jack had never shown them his picture and they accepted that decision.

Anyway before vanishing, Jack told papá that he should apply for U.S. social security as an army veteran, but papá told him that he doubted that Jack's government would want to give him anything or extend any kind of consideration to him because of his past and his former life, which the army itself had condemned and which had led the government to take away his passport and which took him so much effort to get back and then only thanks to a minor official of the U.S. Embassy in Mexico, who for some reason liked papá. But Jack insisted and told papá that he should do everything he could to get it, that he was entitled to it as the U.S. citizen that he still was, despite everything, and that he must try to get it, Jack insisted before leaving. This was the last time that he visited mamá and papá and the last time we saw him.

And yes, papá filed his request and did all the things he had to do and one day he received his first social security check with a note saying that mamá also could apply and that in five years they both would be eligible for all the medical care they needed in the States. This cheered papá up a bit, because he and mamá without saying anything had put up with pain all this time and had cast aside any suspicions of illness and counted the days for the time they would be eligible and could check into a hospital for operations and treatments that wouldn't cost them any money. The monthly social security check is one of the things he waits for from the mailman and one of the things that he counts on in his isolated life in retirement.

Waiting for the mailman is one of papá's main daily activities, and he leaves his bedroom every day around 1 p.m. and goes down the stairs and walks across the courtyard toward the gate, and sometimes he goes out to the street and glances to the left and to the right and waits. Just like papá delivered papers in Flint, the mailman goes around on a bicycle. They get along together so well that the mailman lets papá tease him. He pretends he hasn't given him all his mail, and papá looks through the pouch or acts as if he's searching and the mailman laughs and doesn't get offended because it seems as if they are both co-workers up to something, or that they were or could be co-workers since papá actually knows all about house-to-house deliveries. That's how he learned the names of his neighbors, and he would approach their houses and see how they lived and a neighbor probably told him more than once Come in and have a glass of milk and papá would've accepted this because it was the American thing to do, and he wasn't as much an immigrant as the son of immigrants who wanted to become and became an American, though later, many years later, there were times he was ashamed to be one, though he never thought these were reasons enough to renounce his citizenship.

He's on first-name basis with the mailman and talks to him in the familiar "tú" form and papá does anxiously wait for him not only to get his social security check but also to get his copy of *The Nation* and also the results of a Canadian lottery which he plays and which exasperates him but on which, like in all games, he rests his hopes. Each month he receives lottery cards which he scratches to see his number or picture combination, and one way he wins and the other he loses, but he always loses or when he wins it's either a dollar bill or a little perfumed soap which he never receives. He asks one of us to write to the lottery promoters asking for the soap, but the lottery sponsors are always different — the original promoters do so poorly that they sell the business and the new owners have to pay the winners of the original sponsors. They pay up but papá truly loses his patience and asks another of us to carefully read and explain the rules to him because perhaps he loses because he doesn't play the game right, but the rules are in small print, vague, contradictory and, in the end, unimportant. But papá insists on playing and insists on getting paid his lowliest prize, and it's all a waste because he'll never get back his original investment though it keeps him busy.

Sometimes we think that that's why he's able to go gripe at the state-owned phone company offices or the banks. He puts on his suit, and he's the first to enter since he's been waiting in line for the doors to open since before nine, and he asks to speak to the manager. More often than not they tell him that the manager hasn't arrived yet, or that he's too busy, and they ask him what he wants. That's when papá begins to get ticked off and demands to speak to the manager and won't take no for an answer. When they finally admit him into the main office he presents his complaint to the manager, and if the manager says to him One minute papá bangs his fist on the desk and demands that they listen to him. He loses his temper, and the manager finally gives him an explanation and promises that they won't make the same mistake again and only then does papá stand up and leave though he can't help thinking that they will make the same mistake again. And they do because it's not just a mistake but a big failure in a system that can't seem to be repaired, but for the time being whatever it is gives papá an excuse to lose his temper and complain and demand and yes, this keeps him busy.

Still mamá worries and would like papá to at least go back to playing chess but since his partner died he hasn't played the game again or taken the board out even to look at it because it makes him recall personally not only the General with whom he played chess at home but also Neider, his comrade in the Spanish Civil War, who taught him how to play and who later was killed at his feet by a German shell. All of this must make papá remember these events and that's why he is the way he is and everyone knows how he is, though sometimes he laughs, even bursts out laughing, but that's when mamá gets most frightened and worried. She says that what's just happened doesn't deserve so much laughter, which can be something like the wife of the U.S. president stumbling at a concert in front of celebrities and all of the press and being photographed with her legs up in the air and she's caught in a ridiculous pose. This makes him laugh as hard as when he sees an eighty-year-old president, deposed and in exile for being a corrupt monster, doing physical exercises like lifting his legs in the belief that he is in training, strengthening himself to come back to power and once again to steal and murder. This really amuses him and makes him laugh, but mamá gives him a slight kick under the table so he won't laugh so hard. That's when it seems as if she prefers him to be sad and we're the ones that worry; in these situations we don't know what we should do, whether to laugh real hard like papá or like mamá act composed. Most of the time we react like him and then usually the rest of the family frowns on us like they frown on him and maybe that's why they began to refer to us as being communists like him, because like papá we like it when the stupid manipulations of the U.S. President end in failure.

For a while papá enjoyed or grew visibly proud to hear on the radio or on television or to read in the press what his old friend Yamil Barudi was up to till one awful day he also disappeared like the others who had vanished one at a time. At one point Yamil visited papá in Mexico and had introduced him one at a time in our house to the three Arab princes with whom he was traveling. The five of them talked about going together to the races but we never found out why they never went, and it remained in our minds as a game that had been put off. Yamil Barudi had risen to be nothing less than Saudi Arabia's representative to the United Nations though he was Lebanese or like papá the son of Lebanese immigrants. Papá read and heard how his old friend attacked all the U.S. proposals, and he applauded from his seat and from his retirement. It was as if Yamil was doing what he was doing also in papá's name and by following the course of his life he was kept busy and filled with pride.

The death of the General with whom papá played chess at home and who called us little bastards saddened him and made him give up playing chess. It also made him smile because it had been a somewhat "tender" death for a man like him, who was full of contrasts. No one expected that he could be tender as well as unfriendly, and he died simply because his wife had just passed away. Barely two or three days after he had buried her, he sat down in a chair in his widower's house and died. Well, it was clear that papá's friends were either vanishing or dying one at a time and soon more were gone than were still around. Those that were around were scattered about or like papá isolated for reasons similar to his and everything around him was unavoidably silent and distant and yes, sad, though at times there were other things that could be amusing at the very least.

While all this happened papá still went out every morning with the dog, and they'd walk by the bridge that he could see from the window of his bedroom. Sometimes he'd walk up and down the bridge several times, but he never went under it, even though he asked himself each time if the rich or the poor were the ones who slept under it covered with the dead leaves and the mounds of garbage. The dog wanted to play and papá didn't have the time to do anything under the bridge, and from there he had to go up and down the bridge because the dog would run ahead, barking and jumping. Papá would struggle to keep up with him because, yes, he couldn't throw a ball for the dog to bring back in between his teeth. Yes, papá couldn't make that kind of effort, or else he preferred to save his energy for a good argument with some manager and not waste it on the dog playing a game they hadn't really practiced. Now before going out to take his morning walk, he leaves his gold watch on the little night table, and he puts on an old pair of pants and an old sweater because every day there are more rumors that at all hours and in all corners of the city there are assaults, robberies, and attacks, and papá doesn't want to take any chances and this calms mamá down.

Some of his friends who live in the States and used to visit him in Mexico City, or even sometimes stayed at our house or in the hotel when he still owned it, write or call papá or mamá once in a while, though each day there are fewer of them as they die off one at a time. They say they're coming to Mexico but not to Mexico City and in order to see them to talk and reminisce, they suggest or even invite them to meet in this or that beach resort or city or to come to the Mexico City airport and spend a few hours. Now they can't even spend a single night in the capital, not even to be with papá and mamá, not exactly in Mexico City but in their house with them. But they won't even do this, for they refuse to stay in Mexico City, and then papá or actually mamá answers the letter or the call and tells their friends that they would love to meet them in the airport or in another city or at a beach but they can't. And they can't because papá doesn't want to, since he simply doesn't want to go out anymore nor travel on the highway nor go to some beach resort nor drive across the city to the airport, not even to spend a few minutes with his friends, which are the only friends he has left, and whom he is truly fond of. So the moment passes and they don't see one another and they lose the chance or don't take advantage of the opportunity and mamá regrets it and feels she did all she could but couldn't convince papá, and he goes on with his retirement and, yes, he prefers to sit next to the window and look out at the bridge with a book in his hands.

But toward the end of 1986 his old friend Ed Lending invited him to spend a few days with him in Miami and for several reasons papá accepted. While he was there, he sold another of his lots in Florida to use the money for daily expenses, though it was tough selling property. He had bought the lots to leave them to mamá when he died since his books wouldn't bring in very much money and he had spent a lot to keep the property up. All this time he's been paying taxes and service on the property and paying agents who are trying to sell the lots and who write to him saying No, no one wants to buy your properties because of their location. But this time papá went to see for himself what he could do with them, how he could get rid of them and continue living and supporting mamá and keeping grandma's house, which is the only thing he has — though the only things he really has are his books which say nothing to either mamá or anyone else. In any case, he's not thinking of getting rid of them because he likes rereading them, and he rereads them now more than ever since he can't afford to buy new books, and the Franklin Library he visits hardly has any new books because it can't afford to order new books, and all the old books papá is interested in he has already read and reread.

After meeting with his Florida real estate agent, papá visited his friend Ed in Miami and spent two days with him. Yes, they had a lot to talk about, and papá told mamá upon his return We spoke for hours on end without listening to one another, and he giggled and said Well, that's not quite true and that, yes, they had talked a lot since they hadn't seen each other for a long time. Also, one night after conversing for hours, Ed suddenly uncorked a champagne bottle and in the middle of their talk — hearing and not hearing each other — Ed raised his voice so papá would hear him and told him or asked him Do you know what we're celebrating, and papá said he didn't know. Ed then said Fifty years ago we joined the Abraham Lincoln Brigade and we went to fight in Spain, and they both made a toast and reminisced, and they went on like that until daybreak till they saw, through the window and to the right where the sea was, a huge orange ball that gradually turned into the sun. Papá packed his bags and said goodbye to Ed, returned home and told mamá what he told her.

He spoke with lots of pauses, as he tells things now that he converses, pausing every so often and searching for the right word. When he doesn't find it, he says I've lost my words, since he now says that he forgets everything and it's not that he's forgotten because two or three days later he finds the word he was looking for. Only now it doesn't help him and if he uses it, it would be pointless because this isn't the right word for now. What actually happens is that he uses his vocabulary at the wrong time, but not because he doesn't have vocabulary. So what if he forgets this or that for a long or a short time, what we do know is he has not forgotten what he thought he wanted to forget and hasn't.

Speaking of vocabulary, one Saturday morning a few months ago papá ran into one of us and said I'm glad we've run into each other and he told him that he was out looking for a cobbler to stain his shoes. He was carrying an old pair of shoes inside a plastic bag, and he showed the shoes to the one of us he had met and then asked in English. Honestly tell me how do you say stain in Spanish. He repeated the phrase he had to tell the cobbler several times and when he returned an hour later with his darkened shoes he ran into another one of us and told him in English I visited the cobbler and said to him in Spanish, What will it cost and how long will it take to stain these shoes. When he said the word stain he puckered his face because, yes, he had a hard time pronouncing this verb and he told him that while the cobbler stained the shoes, he took the opportunity to buy himself a vanilla and coffee ice cream with melted chocolate and almond chunks on top because this was his favorite combination and every once in a while he would break his diet to order an ice cream, eat it and be happy.

And that's how papá's lengthy retirement has been going and was going. He had a routine that kept him busy and at times amused him. Though he was often silent and seemed sad, he was actually fine. Sometimes he smiled and a long time had passed since we had seen him cry or even sob and mamá, meanwhile, though she worried, she didn't worry that much. After all, they received social security checks and together with the money from the lots papá was able to sell in Florida, the two of them were getting by okay, and at times they were even comfortable and happy.

And yet one morning several months ago when papá took the dog for a walk by the bridge he forgot to take off the gold watch with our names engraved in back and leave it on his little night table. He told mamá that when he realized he still had it on, he began to worry. At that moment he saw a ragged man approaching from the corner and though it bothered him that a poor person could make him so distrustful, he had whistled for the dog to return home right away. But the dog was having a good time and barked and continued scampering and papá tripped chasing after him. He was very nervous and worried but finally he was able to start walking home with the dog at his side when the ragged man drew close. Papá tried to hurry off while at the same time maintaining his composure, when suddenly a neighborhood patrol car caught up with them and stopped at their side. The two officers opened their doors, and stepped out, and the dog started barking at them. Papá held him by the collar with one hand while one of the officers held one of papá's hands. But at that very moment his partner said Let him go, it wasn't him, and he gave papá a little pat on the back so that he would calm down. The ragged man walked by them not saying a word, of course, and of course not doing anything, and when he was completely out of sight, one of the officers insisted that his partner should let go of papá. This guy finally did, but papá wasn't able to calm himself because among other reasons, the dog wouldn't quit snarling and barking. He couldn't let go of the dog till the officers climbed back into their patrol cars, closed the doors, and drove off at an exaggeratedly fast speed, and papá finally headed home. Mamá was having her breakfast, and he went inside to see her. When he sat down at her side and began to tell her what had happened, he realized that despite or because of everything he wasn't wearing his watch anymore. At that point, before telling the rest of the story to mamá, he dropped his shoulders: they went up and down and nothing could be done about it.

I can't go out any more without someone to protect me, papá said when he had regained his composure, although he would never fully regain it after this. Now more than ever we end up visiting him in the room with the view of the bridge and see him already wearing his robe — long before it gets dark — and saying I don't care if I live or die.

In those days there was a television series commemorating the Spanish Civil War, and papá would lock himself up and ask mamá to join him. She would sit at his side and watch it with him. At times she saw him weep and heard him tell her You can't imagine how many of my friends died there, and mamá would cross her fingers for the show to come to an end and for papá to be at peace again.

The day papá returned home from the funeral of the ex-Ambassador to Mexico from the Spanish Republic in Exile, we were in the yard. He approached us in his dark suit and tie, smiling, and he sat down and drank a cup of coffee. We brought him some of mamá's almond cookies, and we all were about to speak when papá began talking about his friend who had just died. He said it would have been different if he had still been Ambassador when he died, and he expressed his regret that the situation could've allowed the idea of a Spain in Exile to die. The best thing that could've happened was for him to have died in Spain, only of course in a Republican Spain once again. From there he talked about the business side of dying and that during the funeral a friend had told him that he had inquired there and that it was impossible to get a simple pine coffin unless you ordered it ahead of time, and if you hadn't, you had to to buy the readymades which were expensive and ugly and pure business. A wake in a parlor was pure business and to be buried was pure business because you had to buy a plot and it was expensive. Then papá said that he didn't want to contribute to the death business, and that's when he told the husband of one of the females among us that he had a favor to ask. But before asking, he told him for all of us to hear that he had already asked a doctor friend of one of our uncles and that this doctor, though a professor at the University, had told papá yes to the favor he had asked. Time had gone by and he hadn't done anything as far as papá could tell and in any case this doctor had already died and he was asking him now because he was his son-in-law and also taught at the university but not in the Department of Medicine. He assured him that he fully trusted him and that the favor consisted in getting the application or the necessary documents for him to be able to donate his body to the University and in that way avoid contributing to the death business, not to mention that he would be contributing to science and that maybe he would end up saving someone's life since his organs were still in pretty good shape and could be transplanted. Even if he had lost his strength and was hard of hearing, his heart, liver and kidneys were pretty good and he asked the husband of this one of our sisters what did he think, and he asked him that he at least promise right then and there to keep his promise to do all he could for the University to accept his body. He also told us that he had checked with the U.S. Embassy as a citizen of that country and had been told that even though he was a U.S. citizen and had served in his country's army even if only as an ordinary soldier or frozen out and even if he received a social security check and soon be able to take advantage of all the retiree services, the embassy wouldn't be responsible for sending his body to any university in the States and furthermore the U.S. government would not absorb the costs and the university that asked for papá's body would have to cover the costs. That's when we all began to worry and Tito Lovo, the husband of this one of our sisters, said Yes, I promise you to papá to calm him down. He did calm down a bit, though later, while drinking another cup of coffee and eating more of mama's homemade almond cookies, he revived the discussion and said that if his son-in-law didn't get him the appropriate papers to sign in a reasonable amount of time to transfer the body, he would completely forget about the idea though it seemed to him to be most sensible, and he would have to choose another way.

The other thing that papá wanted was that when he felt the right moment had arrived like the wanderer or the stranger in a strange world he's been himself, he would put on the oldest pair of pants and the oldest sweater he has and barefoot — since the two or three pairs of shoes he owns are still good and could be worn by the males among us — without any warning, he's going to get up from his chair by the window, put his glasses on the book that he's reading, and abandon the room that has been practically a house to him. He is going to go down the steps and walk across the patio to the gate, go out to the street and walk toward the bridge that he has been looking at all this time. He will go under it for the first time and will ask himself for the last time whether it is the rich or the poor who sleep under the bridges and beg for alms in the streets, and without answering himself, he will little by little cover himself up with the dead leaves, and provided that he doesn't contribute to — or more importantly doesn't perpetuate — the death business, and provided that he protests about everything till the last moment, he will simply allow himself to die. Yes, he believes that this way he'll be able to die in peace and will once and for all stop being undesirable and dangerous or undesirable or dangerous, covered by dead leaves, and then even though he would never again hear the females among us or the males among us or, in one word, all of us — no matter how childish we seem to be and sound and truly are because we are still looking for the right moment, and even though papá isn't that interested in music — we would sing Papá we need you, Papá we love you, Papá we miss you and really need you, though this last phrase isn't part of the song from the picture with Bette Davis we saw years ago, while papá who had paid for his ticket waited in the theater lobby with an open book in his hands.